Natural Histories

Natural Histories

GUADALUPE NETTEL

translated from the Spanish by
J. T. Lichtenstein

Seven Stories Press
NEW YORK • OAKLAND

Seven Stories Press
140 Watts Street
New York, NY 10013
www.sevenstories.com

College professors may order examination copies of Seven Stories Press titles for
free. To order, visit http://www.sevenstories.com/textbook or send a fax on school
letterhead to (212) 226-1411.

Book design by Elizabeth DeLong

Library of Congress Cataloging-in-Publication Data
Nettel, Guadalupe, 1973- author.
  [Matrimonio de los peces rojos. English]
  Natural Histories / Guadalupe Nettel ; translated by J. T. Lichtenstein.
    pages cm
  ISBN 978-1-60980-551-7 (hardback)
  ISBN 978-1-60980-605-7 (paperback)
  1. Nettel, Guadalupe, 1973---Translations into English. I. Lichtenstein, J. T., 1986
II. Title.
  PQ7298.424.E76M3813 2014
  863'.7--dc23

                              2013050804

This Work has been awarded the International Short Story Award Ribera del
Duero 2013, endowed by the Consejo Regulador de la Denominación de Origen
de Ribera del Duero.

to Ale Oru and Pelo Pegado

All animals know what it is they need, except for man.
—Pliny the Elder

Man belongs to an animal species that when injured can become particularly ferocious.
—Gao Xingjian

Contents

The Marriage of the Red Fish

Our last red fish, Oblomov, died yesterday afternoon. I had a feeling he was going to, having barely seen him move in his round fishbowl for some days. He didn't leap either as he used to for food or to chase the rays of sunlight that brightened his habitat. It was like he was a victim of depression, or its equivalent in the life of a fish in captivity. I came to know very few things about this animal. Very few times I peered through the glass of his bowl and looked him in the eyes and when I did, it wasn't for very long. It pained me to see him there, alone, in his glass container. I very much doubt he was happy. That's what most saddened me when I saw him yesterday, floating like a poppy petal on the surface of a pond. He, on the other hand, had more time, more serenity to spend watching Vincent and me. I am sure that in his way he too felt sorry for us. You tend to learn a lot from the animals you live with, even fish. They are like mirrors that reflect the buried emotions and behaviors we don't dare see.

Oblomov was not the first fish we had in the house, but the third. Before him there were two others of the same color, which I did observe, and which became a fascinating object of study for me. They came one Saturday morning, two months before Lila was born. Pauline, a mutual friend, brought them to us in the same container in which their successor was to die. Vincent and I were very happy to accept the gift. A cat or dog would have been a third wheel in our relation-ship and a nuisance in our apartment, but we liked the idea of sharing our home with another couple. Plus we had heard that red fish bring luck and in those days we were seeking any kind of talisman, be it animal or object, to temper our anxiety about the pregnancy.

We first placed the fish on a small corner table in the living room where the afternoon sun fell. We thought they cheered up the room, which faced the patio behind our building, with the quick movements of their fins and tails. I don't know how many hours I must have spent watching them. A month earlier I had requested maternity leave from the law office where I worked to prepare for the birth of my daughter. It wouldn't be forever, and it wasn't uncommon, but still it troubled me. I didn't know what to do at home. The too-many empty hours filled me with questions about my future.

Winter was at its worst and just the thought of getting dressed to face the icy wind was enough to dissuade me from going out for a walk. I preferred to stay home, reading the newspaper or getting things ready for Lila's arrival, turning the tiny study into a bedroom for her. On the other hand Vincent was spending more time in the office than ever. He wanted to make the most of these last few months to get ahead on his projects before the baby was born. Reasonable enough, but I missed him, even when we were together. He felt distant, lost in his busy schedule and in his professional worries where there was no place for me. Often, waiting for him to come home from work, I sat and watched the fishes' sometimes slow and measured, sometimes frantic or terrorized comings and goings. I learned to tell them apart, not just by the nearly imperceptible differences in the colors of their scales, but by their behavior and the way they moved, searched for food. There was nothing else in the fishbowl. No stone, no cavity in which to hide. The fish always saw each other, and every act by one, every rising to the surface and circling of the glass, inevitably affected the other. Hence the impression of dialogue watching them gave me.

Unlike Oblomov, those fish never had names. We referred to them as the male and the female. Despite their strong resemblance it was possible to distinguish them by the robust build of the former and because his scales shined brighter than his companion's. Vincent watched them much less, but they inspired a curiosity in him as well. I'd tell him of the things I thought I'd discovered about them and he enjoyed hearing about the happenings in the lives of the extended family staying with us. I remember one morning, while I was at the kitchen counter making coffee, he pointed out to me that one of them—possibly the male—had opened its fins and they now looked bigger, as if doubled, and full of colors.

"And the female?" I asked, coffeepot in hand. "Is she prettier too?"

"No. She's still the same, but she's barely moving," Vincent said, his face pressed to the glass of the fishbowl. "Maybe he's courting her."

That day we went to the outdoor market on Boulevard Richard-Lenoir. A favorite weekend activity of ours. The snow had disappeared and instead of the eternal rain we could feel the sun's presence in the sky. We enjoyed ourselves shopping, but the morning didn't end on the same note. We were ready to head home, loaded down with bags of food, when I got the urge to ask if we could buy oranges and Vincent refused so sharply it felt like an insult.

"They're so expensive this time of year," he argued untruthfully. "We can't afford it. It's like you have no sense of the expenses we'll have once the baby is born. You can't go on squandering money like always."

Maybe it was the hormones. Pregnant woman often get upset over nothing. But what's certain is that in less than five minutes it felt like dark and menacing clouds had engulfed my life. All men cater to their pregnant wives' wishes, I thought. Some people believe these inexplicable cravings in fact reflect the baby's nutritional needs. What was wrong with Vincent? How could he just refuse like that to buy a few simple oranges? I tried to make it home without getting caught up in an argument. But after a few steps I had to sit down on a bench to rest. My coat didn't close around me anymore and a sweater that to me seemed old and hideous was poking out from its black edge. I felt my eyes fill with tears. Vincent noticed as well but he wasn't about to let it go.

"You're impossible to please," he said. "We came to the market so you'd be happy and you get like this over something stupid. Unbelievable."

It took a lot of restraint not to get up and go buy the oranges with my own money, but my happiness did not return the entire weekend. When we got home the male of the fishbowl still had his gills erect. His seductive behavior seemed arrogant to me. The female swam with drooping fins and her movements, listless compared to his, made me sad.

On Monday I left the house early. I sat down in the brasserie on the corner and ordered a tall orange juice. I also had a café crème and a croissant and paid with our joint credit card. Afterward I went to a bookstore and bought a novel, then spent an hour trying on clothes in the store on rue des Pyrénées that carries large sizes and found the perfect sweater to replace mine. I went back home midday, just before lunchtime. Once inside, I went directly to the living room and peered into the fishbowl, as if consulting an oracle: the male still had his fins unfolded but now his companion also exhibited a physical change. All along her body two dull brown horizontal lines had appeared. I cooked pasta with eggplant and ate it standing up, looking out the kitchen window at two workers doing repairs on the facing building. I then diligently washed the dirty pot and utensils. Afterward I went out for a walk through the neighborhood and ended up at the library. I felt a pull to go in, but it closed early on Mondays so I went back home and read my novel while waiting for Vincent. When he came in I showed him the lines on the female's body, which had me a little scared. But to him they looked insignificant.

"Those lines are barely noticeable and I don't think they mean anything. I'm not even sure she didn't have them before," he said.

We ate dinner in silence, reheated rice that had been in the freezer for months. Vincent did the dishes and went into the living room where he worked until dawn. Without a word to him I started putting up the teddy bear wallpaper border in the baby's room, a chore we'd been meaning to do for weeks but that neither of us had gotten around to. I just wanted to take care of one of the infinite things we had to do. True, the result wasn't as tidy as I'd wanted it to be, but it wasn't disastrous either. Vincent, however, saw it as provocation. He insisted that I had intentionally put it up unevenly to make him feel guilty.

"You could have asked me to do it. I don't know why you keep trying to be a victim lately."

Tuesday morning we ate a breakfast of tea and toast

like two polite strangers, but as soon as he left for work I went down to the brasserie full of resentment and had another orange juice. Then I walked to the library in a light rain. In my days as a student I had gone there often, but hadn't been in a while. My office was on the Rive Gauche, and whenever some query arose that could not be answered from the Internet I would go to the National Library. Unlike that one, which was almost always empty, the library in my neighborhood was full of teenagers like the one I had been in high school: slightly older kids who spoke to each other by yelling and roared with laughter. People who ate in cafeterias and whose only concerns were passing their exams and making the money from their parents or the government last the month. Normally, or at least for the past few years, people of that age made me feel a certain condescension. So I was surprised that morning to feel envy. I was about to push open the main door when one of them, wearing a red and white scarf around his neck, bumped into my stomach.

"Sorry, ma'am," he said, barely slowing down.

More than my pregnant state, it was his falsely contrite tone that made our age difference so obvious—to me anyway.

Once inside I headed toward the Natural Science section and found the *Encyclopedic Dictionary of Marine Animals* and searched for our fish. I discovered that they belonged to the *Betta splendens* species, also known as "Siamese fighting fish." They are originally from Asia, where they often inhabit stagnant waters.

Experts classify them as a labyrinth fish because of a rhizome-shaped bronchial organ on the top of their head that allows them to breath a small amount of air at the surface of the water. According to the article, one of their most notorious characteristics was their trouble with cohabitation. The dictionary did not abound in details about that or about how to look after them. If I wanted advice on their care I'd have to look elsewhere. It didn't mention anything about the stripes that had appeared on the female's flanks, either.

I looked at other books about fish and chose a few to bring home. I filled out the cards to sign up and check them out. As silly as it sounds, it thrilled me to be using the library again. It was raining hard when I tried to leave to go home, so I paused a moment by the bookshelves in the entrance where they had newspaper supplements and magazines from that month available to the public. I glanced over them, unable to make up my mind which to read. They were all there, from *Magazine Littéraire* to *Marie-Claire*. The cover of the latter displayed the title of an article that seemed to be speaking directly to me: *Pregnancy. Why do they leave us right in this moment?* I realized that the rain could last for hours and was contemplating going home anyway when my phone rang. Vincent, apologizing for being selfish. He had gone to the apartment so we could have lunch together. "I stopped at the trattoria you like and bought lasagna. I also got you oranges." When he heard I was at the library he offered to come for me. We returned home arm in arm beneath his huge umbrella, blue with white clouds. The remnants of breakfast were still on the kitchen counter. Vincent took the delicacies from his bag and warmed them in the microwave. While we ate and he served himself two glasses of wine, I told him what I'd discovered about our pets. We laughed because they had been from Pauline and were as eccentric and complex as she. After lunch we made love. One of the few times we did during the pregnancy. It was a quick and tender fuck, but not without desire. Vincent said goodbye to me in bed with a kiss and went back to the office. A few minutes later, while getting dressed in front of the mirror, I noticed a brown line running straight down the middle of my stomach.

I spent the afternoon reading on the couch and watching the fishbowl. While they were not scientific works, the books I had borrowed from the library offered more practical information than had the *Encyclopedic Dictionary*. Both were intended for a younger audience, or at least one not very well versed on the topic. In one of them I found information on *Betta splendens*. Its author gave details about their care and reproduction; for example, he said the male's expanding operculum indicated his desire to mate, and he can become violent if rejected. But that wasn't the worst of it. The books described the fish as highly combative; it's why they are commonly referred to as "fighters." In some countries people even use them as fighting animals and enter them into a ring, just like how the Western world bets on cockfights. Reading this I felt something like embarrassment. The feeling you get when you discover the dark facets of those you know well without their consent. Did I really want to know all this about our fish? I realized I did. It was better to be aware and avoid any kind of accident, as far as possible. The book advised against having two males in the same tank, no matter how large. There was a better chance, on the other hand, of a male and a female surviving together, as long as they had enough space. Five liters, at least. I looked at our fishbowl; the amount of water was absurd. "When in distress or danger," the author continued, "*Bettas* develop horizontal stripes, contrasting with the color of their body."

When my husband came in, I had been asleep on the couch for over an hour. Vincent closed the books, careful to mark the open pages, and with caresses woke me up so I'd go to bed. But before going back to sleep, I tried to share with him what I had read about our fish.

"It's dangerous to leave them in that bowl," I said to him. "They could really get hurt. What if they kill each other?"

I made him promise to move them into an aquarium, with oxygen and some stones where they could hide when they didn't feel like showing their faces. He humored me, amused.

"You've become obsessed with this," he said. "When you go back to work you should specialize in animal rights."

It was several days before we removed the fish from their container. Tense days for them but also for us, as Vincent didn't relish the idea of cluttering our living room with an aquarium.

"It's going to look like a Chinese restaurant!" he let slip out once, defeated and knowing full well there would be no negotiating on the matter.

I always kept an eye on them whenever I was home, as if with that look, severe and exact, an imminent confrontation could be averted. I of course felt solidarity with her. I could feel her fear and her anxiety at being cornered, feel her need to hide. Fish are perhaps the only domestic animals that don't make noise. But they taught me that screams can be silent. Vincent adopted an ostensibly more neutral position, betrayed nonetheless by the humorous comments he dropped now and again: "What's wrong with the female? Is she against reproduction?" or "Keep calm, brother, even if you're getting impatient. Remember that laws today are made by and for women."

Meanwhile the baby was floating in amniotic fluid inside my belly. At the last visit to the obstetrician we'd been told she was "engaged" and that was what I was feeling in my hips. Sometimes, in the silence of the afternoon, I'd hear my sacrum bones crunching. The thirty-fifth week had passed. It was a question of days. The more I thought about it, the greater was my need for everything to be in order in the apartment, and in truth, everything was except for the relationship between our pets. So I insisted on buying the fish tank that weekend. The home we picked out for our *Bettas* was a green aquarium that could hold up to ten liters of water, as the book recommended, tall but narrow at the base so it would fit on our bookcase. It was Vincent's idea to put it there, where it would take up an entire shelf but not a single centimeter of living room surface space. We had to relocate several adaptations of *The Civil Code* for the Siamese fighting fish who had thus far, perhaps aware of our peacekeeping intentions, remained calm. In truth I did relax when, after several failed attempts and a technician's visit, the fish were settled in and the female had, at last, a cave she could hide in.

Lila was born the same week, a few blocks from the apartment at the Clinique des Bleuets, one of the few public maternity wards that do water births. I remember Vincent's horrified face when it was suggested to us. "How perfect," he said, alluding to our pets. To me, however, it didn't seem like such a bad idea. I'd heard many times that it's less traumatic for babies to be born underwater than to enter the world on a hospital bed. I would have liked to try it. But opposing Vincent was the last thing I wanted to do right then. Lila came into the world at nine p.m. after eight hours of labor of which seven transpired in a generic hospital room that smelled of disinfectant. As I suffered the pains of contraction I tried to imagine that, instead of there, I was in the ocean in Brittany, and immense waves were pummeling my body. Later, when they took the baby away to run some tests and left me in the recovery room to rest, I overheard the nurses who had attended the birth talking. One said:

"Baby Chaix's birth was fine but I couldn't believe how tense her parents were. Just being with them was exhausting."

It bothered me that they would talk about us like that, while I lay on a cot, naked beneath the sheets, separated from them only by a white curtain. However, beyond their indiscretion, their distanced discussion of the event interested me. After all, I thought, maybe they weren't wrong.

During the pregnancy and, I believe, for my entire life, I had imagined those first days at home follow-ing the birth of a child to be the most romantic and marvelous days imaginable for a couple. And while I don't know exactly what these days are generally like for everyone else, I can say that in my case, they were not like that at all. Adapting to the lack of sleep and the delicate task of taking care of a baby demanded nearly superhuman strength. Never before had I understood so clearly the importance of sleep, nor why prisoners who are to be interrogated are often tortured first by being denied it. It was hard for me to imagine peo-ple going through this generation after generation, as if being someone's parent were the most obvious and logical thing in the world. My husband and I were both equally afraid of harming the baby. Bathing her, dressing her, cleaning her umbilical cord were feats that filled us with self-doubt. It seemed cruel to me to have her sleep in her own bed right away, after spending nine months attached to my body. But for Vincent it was a basic rule of survival. We tried both, but either way, waking up every two hours—that was how often she needed to be fed and changed—became unbearable. We were like two irritable zombies locked inside an apartment. We barely spoke during those days. We took turns sleeping and we always felt like the other one got more of it. I pushed myself to the ends of my limits, but it was never enough. My husband would indirectly accuse me of not taking care of the baby like an exemplary mother and I reproached him his recriminations. This whole time, he had been the one in charge of the fish tank.

Things got better when Vincent went back to work. True, I had to take care of the baby for the entire day, but I didn't have to argue about whether she was crying because she was hungry or because she was cold. It wasn't long before I found a rhythm, a routine that began with breastfeeding her in the morning, changing her diaper and often her clothes, walking her in the carriage if it wasn't raining, more breastfeeding, some motor skill development exercises, bath, etc. True, Lila sometimes slept well, which I took advantage of to cook, wash clothes and dishes, tidy the apartment up a bit. But that's not how it was most of the time. According to the pediatrician, she had terrible colic, and though normal for her age, it meant I'd have to comfort her somehow, by rocking her, singing to her, lulling her to sleep.

My husband usually came home during bath time. He would dry her, put her pajamas on, and get her ready for bed. After her last feeding he would try to get her to sleep. It took him hours; we ate dinner late and always exhausted. Neither of us had the energy for conversation. Once in a while I would make an effort, asking him questions about work or telling him something amusing I'd seen while out walking with Lila in the carriage. But it was useless. Vincent would just smile. And I won't even go into sex. We'd had it maybe a couple of times since the birth, in a state of somnambulism. Like everyone, Vincent had his insecurities and one of them was about being a bad parent. I remember one time he was trying, in vain, to lull her to sleep, and I offered to take over. I only wanted for us to eat early and, for once, a meal that hadn't gone cold. He took it as an insult.

"Now you're going to tell me I do this badly too? You should learn to shut your mouth. I don't waste my time pointing out your ineptitudes and countless mistakes."

I tried to explain my point of view but it was no use. The discussion rapidly got more and more intense and didn't end until my husband left, slamming the door. I was left rocking Lila, who that night took a little longer to fall asleep.

Many people came to visit us in that first month. Some of my friends and family members offered to stay with me a few hours while Vincent was at work. Most of them, however, showed up on weekends when they would find us both. It was a strange period in which we saw people we hadn't in a long time. Everyone brought gifts for our daughter, clothes, toys, and new or used appliances they themselves hadn't even bought and which they no longer needed. Neither my husband

nor I dared refuse the gifts; neither of us knew where
to put them. Lila's closet was tiny. One Sunday morning Vincent announced we were not going to accept
any visitors. While I understood the decision and deep
down agreed with it, it bothered me that he decided
for us both, and I told him so. We didn't speak a word
to each other the entire morning. In the afternoon
Vincent, with the same despotism as earlier, worked on
separating out the gifts he deemed useless. I remained
locked in the bedroom with Lila under the pretext of
taking a nap, and in those quiet moments I attentively
observed the fish. How were they doing? What events
had transpired in their subaquatic life while we were so
busy with our own? They had remained calm all this
time, or at least that's the sense I got. If there had been
some friction or fighting between them, it had gone
unnoticed. I wondered if the female had been in heat
again. I saw then such wisdom in nature: this animal
was aware—god knows how—that it wasn't a good idea
to get pregnant, not even in a place as ample and well
equipped as hers. I also wondered if it was the specimen with whom she shared it that deterred her or if
under no circumstance, not even with a different mate,
would she have agreed to procreate.

That same Sunday my mother called from Bordeaux
to announce she was coming to meet her granddaughter. She was thinking of spending a week in Paris and
wanted to know if she could stay with us, or if we
would rather she stayed in a hotel. I told her I would
check with Vincent and call her the next morning to

let her know, and then passed the phone to my husband so he could say hello. But he didn't want to wait until Monday to give his opinion. "I'm sorry, mother-in-law dear, but this time you must stay somewhere else." Hearing the irritated tone in which he spoke to my mother, I lost it.

"Who do you think you're talking to, you *goujat*!" I screamed at him as soon as he hung up, hurling one of the toys he had decided to keep at his head. The screaming woke Lila, who started crying at the top of her lungs, making the atmosphere even tenser. When at last I was able to calm her down I went to bed, certain I had crossed an impassible line. That night Vincent slept on the couch and I in our bed, the baby in my arms.

Mom stayed at Hôtel de la Paix, a few blocks from our building. As soon as Vincent left for work, she came to the apartment and stayed with me the whole day, helping me with the laundry, the cleaning, and taking care of Lila. Rarely had we been so close. We would put Lila down to sleep before seven p.m. and drink tea while we spoke about marriage and its difficulties or the great challenges other family members have had to face. My mother had had three children and survived it. For once, I was completely open to her advice. Every evening she left before Vincent came home. What's more, I noticed she did everything she could to erase all evidence of her presence from the apartment. For his part Vincent took advantage of her visit to stay late at the office and get ahead on his

work. Right after Mom left I would settle in to eat dinner in front of the TV. I no longer watched the fish.
Observing the aquarium for a long time made me sick.
The life of those two conflicting beings saddened me.
When he got home my husband would find me in bed,
either with a book or having just fallen asleep. I realize
it wasn't the ideal situation for a couple but at least we
were peaceful, and I would have given anything for that
period to go on indefinitely. On Saturday at around ten
a.m. my mother and I went to pick up Dad from the
train station. He came to spend a few days with us,
and of course to meet his granddaughter. That weekend it was unseasonably warm for Paris in March. We
spent a lot of time outside, walking through the Marais
and the Place des Vosges. On Sunday we took Lila to
the Luxembourg Gardens for her first time. Vincent
didn't come with us on any of these outings. He wasn't
even kind enough to say goodbye to my parents. Our
relationship didn't get any better after they left. He
still returned home after dinnertime and that routine,
which began as an exception, became the norm.

This was around the time my maternity leave came
to an end. I called the office to negotiate my return to
work and, after some evasiveness, I was told that with
the arrival of my temporary replacement, apparently an
efficient and highly qualified young woman, things had
become complicated. It was never explicitly expressed,
but it was clear to me they didn't want a lawyer with
a different set of priorities. I asked for a meeting with
the director of the firm, but he was away. From then

on domestic life seemed insufferable. I no longer saw my time at home as the transitional phase into working motherhood, but rather a kind of house arrest that could go on forever. I felt unhappy and most of all, alone. It was almost Easter and travel agencies were bombarding viewers with images in ads on bus stops, in the streets, and on the television of happy families vacationing on beaches in the Caribbean or the Indian Ocean. Vincent had a week off and I suggested that we get out of Paris. When I stopped talking, he looked at me as if I had said something crazy.

"Our bank accounts are empty," he said. "And we don't even know if you're going back to work."

I then suggested we take a trip to the Southeast and stay at my parents' place.

"You go and take the baby. It would be good for you to get some sun and for me to stay home and get some sleep."

I didn't hear a drop of sarcasm in this remark, and so I agreed to his suggestion.

Bordeaux was a veritable oasis. For the entire week Lila and I spent there, from morning until dinnertime, my parents took care of absolutely everything. I slept like I hadn't in months and recovered a great deal from the accumulated fatigue. My siblings also came to our parents' home with their numerous children. We swam in the pool and on Easter Sunday, following the English tradition, we went hunting for chocolate eggs. Vincent called almost every afternoon to ask about his daughter. Over the phone his voice sounded affectionate and caring, like in the years before her birth. He told me we did well to take a break from each other. In these idyllic surroundings I was able to forget about the law office and I felt truly happy. But too soon it was time to go back. I had no obligation to do so, or even any desire to recoup my work or my daily life. My parents were delighted to have us there. If I went home it was for Vincent. He really wanted to embrace his wife and daughter—at least he said he did—and I for things to be good between us. When the train pulled out of the station and I saw my parents waving through the window, I struggled not to burst into tears.

Vincent came to pick us up in the car. Despite all his smiling, I saw he was nervous. It must have been about nine. It was raining, of course. I remember the light from the streetlamps reflecting on the pavement. Lila was sleeping in her car seat. After asking the obligatory questions—how have you been? how was the trip?—he announced he had something to tell me before we got home.

"It's about the fish," he said. "Two days ago they had a fight and both of them are hurt pretty badly."

He then gave me the details: Friday morning he had found them floating on the top of the tank.

"I have no clue what to do with them. The only thing I could think of was to separate them. I took the male out with the net and put him in the fishbowl Pauline gave us. A specialist is coming tomorrow."

"Was she in heat, do you know?" I asked, trying to

imagine the reasons. "Did you see a dark stripe on her body?"

But Vincent hadn't seen the colorful fins unfolding the way they had the first time.

Never in all the years I lived in that apartment had I seen it so bleak. It smelled like the fish tank was giving off a rotten stench. The fish did look hurt, but much less so than what I had imagined on the way home, listening to Vincent's account.

What made me most sad that night and the following days was seeing our fish apart. I got the sense that the distance affected them too, and they were missing each other.

"How is it possible in an aquarium so big and beautiful they weren't able to live in peace?" I asked my husband one afternoon, as we were watching the male swimming in circles like a lunatic in the old container, now located on the kitchen counter.

"Maybe it's not a question of space," he responded, "but of their nature. They are *Bettas*, remember."

I realized he had given the matter a lot of thought.

"Other fish," he went on, "feel free in very small bowls. To them they are universes, bright and full of color. To them, each beam of sunlight represents a world of possibilities. *Betta* fish on the other hand may see the biggest bowl as very small. They never have enough space and they always feel threatened, even by their mate. It is with all that pressure on them that they interpret the other's nature. I'm not making this up; I read it in one of the books you took out of the library and, by the way, haven't returned yet. Do you know how much the late fee increases every day?"

"It's a drama," I said, completely serious. "I'm convinced our fish love each other, even though they can't live together."

How did I come to this conclusion? Even I didn't know. I thought a bit about our pair of fish. I wondered by what criteria had they been selected at the pet shop to share the container given to Pauline. It had probably been nothing but chance and their being opposite sexes. Perhaps they had been born in the same aquarium and therefore knew each other from before. Or maybe they had never seen the other before being placed in that round fishbowl they had so intimately shared. Could one speak of destiny in the fish world?

I know it sounds foolish when put like this, but my fish suffered by being separated, of that I am absolutely sure. I could sense it as distinctly as I had earlier sensed her fear and her companion's arrogance. I told myself that most likely in living together, even with the female's refusal to reproduce, they had developed a kind of affection or emotional dependency. Hence the gloominess that had been manifest in them ever since the day of the fight.

For several days our male was confined to less than five liters of water and without a single rock to hide behind. We had decided to keep him there while we figured out what to do with them. But my husband continued to stay late at the office and so in the entire week we didn't find a single moment in which to discuss the fate of our fish. On Thursday I brought it up at dinner. Vincent threw me with his response:

"Actually, I think it's an aberration for us to decide for them. It's like being sent to family court."

Rather than a joke, I realized the comment was an evasion. Deep down I wasn't surprised. He'd been slipping away for months.

By Friday I couldn't take it anymore and acted recklessly. I grabbed Pauline's bowl in both hands and with a big splash returned the fish to the matrimonial tank. I then brought my face close to the glass to watch what would happen. After the whirlpool, the male swam downward, to just a few centimeters from the bookshelf. Once there, he stopped moving. The female acted as if nothing had happened. Little by little his mobility returned to him, as did his old habits. He spent a lot of time among the algae plants on the bottom, until the food appeared at the surface of the water. Then he rose like a torpedo, faster than his mate, and devoured as much food as his stomach would allow.

The firm director's solution to my situation was to extend my maternity leave, by dint of another paid leave. To qualify I had to sign a letter claiming I was suffering from postpartum depression. The medical diagnosis they would obtain themselves. I cannot describe how insecure it all made me. The arrangement demonstrated the director's goodwill and complete disregard for my professional performance. Thinking about it a little, it was obvious I wouldn't have worked there for more than four years had I been a bad lawyer. However, knowing that was not enough; it didn't free me from the feeling of having been treated unfairly. At one point I considered the possibility of suing them for sexism, but I didn't have the energy to enter into such a lengthy and uncertain trial. Vincent thought the deal wasn't so bad; the sum they offered was barely less than my salary.

"Think of it as a six-month vacation," he said, trying to convince me. "Meanwhile, you can look for something else. You'll find a better job, you'll see."

The medical diagnosis ultimately turned into a reality, or just about. I did not suffer, of course, from postpartum depression, but rather from profound discouragement and a permanent bad mood. Oddly enough Vincent started showing the same symptoms, even though he had not given birth or lost his job. Had it been a greater misfortune that had befallen us—the death of a parent, a serious illness (ours, or the baby's), the actual loss of our financial resources—perhaps then the jolt would have been enough to bring us closer, or at least make us see things from a different perspective. As it were, in those stagnant waters in which Vincent and I moved, our relationship continued on its gradual course toward putrefaction. We never laughed anymore, or enjoyed ourselves at all. The most positive emotion I was able to feel toward him in several weeks was *appreciation* every time he made dinner or stayed home to take care of Lila so I could go out to the movies with a friend.

It was a blessing, his relieving me. I adored my daughter and overall delighted in her company. But I also needed to have moments by myself and in silence, moments of freedom and escape in which I could reclaim, even if only for a couple of hours, my individuality. The world had shifted ever since we became three and it was amazing how, in this new configuration, parenting consumed what remained of our coupling. Compared to a river or even a small pond, an aquarium, no matter how large, is a space still too small for beings dissatisfied and inclined toward unhappiness, such as *Betta splendens.* Some people have similar minds. There is not space enough therein for happy thoughts or lovely versions of reality. This is how we were in the following months, seeing always the gloomiest side of life, neither fully appreciating nor delighting in our baby and the wonder of her existence, not to mention the infinite inconsequential events—the sun coming out, our health, how lucky we were to have each other.

At the end of May, when you began to feel the heat even at night, Lila got an intestinal infection that gave her a fever of almost 104. Vincent called from the office several times asking after his daughter. He was stuck in a hearing and couldn't come home.

"I'll have to stay late tonight," he had said, "but don't worry, as soon as I come home I'll take care of her and you can sleep."

I had the phone in one hand and with the other I

was submerging the baby in a plastic bathtub, hoping to avoid the use of antipyretics. I was too upset to analyze the tone of his voice or the loud noises in the background. But I can say that, despite my many attempts to get in touch with him, my husband did not call again. Nor did he even send a text to let me know he was alive. His silence went on until six in the morning. In the meantime, I was able to get Lila's fever down and she had been sound asleep since midnight. I waited, troubled, pacing the apartment until at last I heard the sound of the key in the lock.

"I was so worried about you," I told him, honestly. "Where have you been?"

Vincent explained that after the hearing, the guys in his office had gone out to celebrate the end of an awful week. According to him, he had planned to stay out for only a half an hour and then go home, but the drinks had managed to dwindle his willpower.

"I didn't hear you call. There was no signal."

Once the anxiety that something bad had happened to him subsided, an uncontainable wrath awoke in me, charged with all the frustration that had built up over the months. Without a word I began to break, one after another, the plates and the vase on the table.

"You're crazy!" he yelled, trying in vain to get me to stop and think. "Stop it!"

His insults and reprimands did nothing but infuriate me more.

The next day Vincent moved into Lila's room and the baby began sleeping with me every night. It could even be said that in that moment we stopped being husband and wife and became roommates. Vincent didn't come home until dawn several times in two weeks. One morning he didn't come home at all, not even to change his clothes. My mood oscillated between resentment and bottomless sadness. I never stopped wondering if we were going to get out from this and, if not, what other options we had. For me, I couldn't imagine any.

Unlike us, the fish remained calm this entire time, not initiating any disputes. I was taking care of the aquarium those days. Heat as much as worry drew me from bed very early in the morning, before Lila and Vincent woke up, and I would begin circling my own container. One day, with no forewarning, not even a sign, I found the female floating on the top of the aquarium. Her fins were ripped and one eye was out of its socket. Her appearance left little room for doubt. She was dead. The male was also injured but he was still able to move among the algae at the bottom. Without a word I went over to the open window and pulled up the metal blinds to get some fresh air. The inside patio of our apartment looked like a rat's nest. Below, a couple of students were packing their things into a moving truck. I don't know how long I stood there, watching their movements and their excited faces. I didn't hear the shower or the coffeepot that Vincent had turned on. I realized he was awake when he walked in front of me, heading out the door. When he saw I was crying he came over and kissed me on the cheek.

"I'm leaving," he said. "I'm going to be late. We'll talk about all this later"

When Lila turned three months old she was accepted into the day care on rue Saint Ambroise. She'd be there from eight in the morning until four-thirty. A true liberation. For her first day we both went to drop her off. On our way back we passed by the pet shop in République. I asked Vincent if we could stop and buy another *Betta*.

"It would have to be another male," he said, "I hate the idea of replacing the female so soon. Besides, it wouldn't be a bad thing if someone taught that brute a lesson."

"Better to get one that's phlegmatic instead of combative," I said. "A fish with no initiative and indifferent to everything."

We searched among the shop's specimens and chose a red *Betta* with blue fins. We named him Oblomov in the hope that his name would have some positive influence on his temperament. I wondered about this resolve of ours, mine and Vincent's, to keep buying *Bettas*. Why did we not, after that terrible ordeal, find a more amicable species? I suppose what we really wanted was a companion for our widower, not another animal that would be pointing out his faults, all that he was not nor could ever be because of his nature. We decided to leave the new one in a different fishbowl. We had heard that two male *Bettas* living in separate habitats from which they are able to see the other compete by displaying the full range of colors their genes allow them to develop. Oblomov seemed to flourish in his little container, but that was not the case for our widowed fish. Every day he got worse, and in two weeks he was found, just like his old mate, floating on the surface of the tank. After his death we dismantled the aquarium and brought it to the basement. To fill the empty space we returned to the bookshelf my many editions of *The Civil Code*, arranging them as they had been before.

Oblomov remained in his glass bowl, located once again in the little corner table in the living room. Neither Vincent nor I was interested in observing his development or behaviors. We fed him, unsystematically, from time to time. It was around then when I decided to leave and go to Bordeaux. I'd look for work, and when I found it I would move there and live with Lila in an apartment I imagined to be very spacious and not far from the city center. In the meantime I would live with my parents. I spoke to Vincent about it. He could come see Lila whenever he wanted. Perhaps, with the distance between us, things would work themselves out and he would decide to move there too. We said this and other lies I no longer remember. As we spoke, I kept looking over at the red fish circling his bowl, counterclockwise.

I finished packing up my books yesterday morning. Scatterbrained as I was, I included those from the library. I stuck my winter clothes in the metal trunk that had for many years served as a table in an even smaller apartment. In the afternoon, before picking Lila up from daycare, I looked over the books I was going to leave behind because it had never been clear whose they were. I went back and forth between my bedroom and the library countless times. Oblomov had died by the time I was finished. Nobody is surprised Vincent and I are separating. I realize it's a catastrophe everyone saw coming, like the economic collapse of a small country or the death of someone terminally ill. We alone had clung for months to the possibility of a change we didn't even know how to bring about, nor was it in our nature to see through. Nobody made us get married. No unknown hand grabbed us from our family aquariums and placed us in this apartment without our consent. We chose each other for reasons that, at least at the time, felt compelling. The reasons we are leaving each other are much less clear, but equally irrevocable.

War in the Trash Cans

I've been a biology professor at the Universidad de Valle de México for over ten years. I specialize in insects. Some people in my field of research have pointed out to me that when I'm in the laboratory or lecture hall I almost always keep to the corners of the room. It's like when I'm walking along a street; I feel safer if I'm near a wall. Though I can't explain exactly why, I've begun to think it's a habit born of the depths of my nature. My fascination for insects emerged at a young age, when I was about eleven and passing from childhood into adolescence. My parents had recently split up, and as neither one of them was psychologically sound enough to be responsible for the mistake they had engendered together, they decided to send me to live with my mom's older sister, my aunt Claudine, who had managed to build a functional family with two disciplined, tidy, and studious sons. I knew their house well. It was part of a middle-class housing complex with American dreams, as my dad would say. Very different from the place where I'd been born and had spent eleven long years. My house and my aunt's were opposite in every way. We lived in a crumbling section of Colonia Roma, in one of those apartments known today as "lofts" and in those days as "artists studios." Though it actually looked more like a photographer's dark room, for the fabrics—from India, mostly—that kept the sun out; my mom suffered from constant migraines and couldn't stand being exposed to light for very long. In contrast, my aunt and uncle's house had enormous windows, and also a garden where my cousins played Ping-Pong. Whereas in our family all three of us shared household cleaning duty—a duty none of us ever really fulfilled—my aunt employed a kind and quiet maid who lived with her mother in a room up on the roof terrace. Isabel and Clemencia. Once I'd settled into my aunt's house, those two women taught me more things than I'd learned in an entire year at school. Which wasn't surprising, considering that my parents' fighting and screaming had worked on me like a hole punch, perforating my brain. Any information that wasn't indispensable to my survival, such as long division with decimals and mitosis and meiosis, filtered through the holes and became lost forever in oblivion.

I imagine with gratitude how strenuous it must have

been for them to travel to my aunt's house together that January morning. They didn't even stay for the drink offered them, and that was something they never refused. They left my two suitcases in the foyer and made their goodbyes there. The night before, my dad had explained to me that he and my mom thought very differently about many subjects, such as my education. He also assured me that sooner or later things would work themselves out and I'd be able to move in with one of them and spend vacations with the other, like all the other kids with divorced parents at my school whom I'd been observing with curiosity, like you would the victim of a civil war, for some time. Mom didn't say anything. I remember her that night, sitting on a pillow in her favorite position, her legs folded into a triangle and her chin resting on her knees. My parents did not expand upon that explanation on the way to the housing complex. They greeted my aunt and uncle without looking them in the eyes and ordered me, in front of them, to behave myself and do as I was told. After that, without even saying when they'd come for me or at least come visit, they got into the car and disappeared.

My aunt Claudine took me by the hand and led me to what would be my room, from then on. It was a tiny room on the roof terrace between the maid's room where Isabel and Clemencia lived and the staircase leading down to the kitchen. In a hushed tone my aunt apologized for putting me in such an inhospitable place, but my coming had been a surprise and there were no free rooms in the house. I didn't think it was

so bad. I'd always been an observant child and I recognized the advantages of living in a structured house.
It was the first time I had my own room, as space in
my parents' studio was divided only by folding screens
and paper curtains. When she left me alone, I locked
the door and drew the curtains. I moved my bed and
took my clothing out of the suitcase and arranged it in
the dresser drawers, as if moving in. While helping me
pack, my mother had assured me that I would only stay
at my aunt and uncle's a little while, and so it didn't
make sense for me to bring all my belongings. "Maybe
your father and I will reconcile," I remember her saying, stammering like she always did. Still, I preferred
to deal with this change as something definitive. That
afternoon my cousins, a bit older than me, came up to
say hi with a suspicious show of brotherliness I didn't
see again for months, and then went back to their
respective activities until dinnertime. It was January,
but no longer cold. In my memory, that weekend is
like a peaceful haven. It surprised me that there existed
a place where the only sounds of arguing voices came
from soap operas, drifting out of the windows of the
maid's room.

I barely knew my aunt Claudine, and her husband
even less. She was exactly what my mom called a "traditional woman," that is, a lady, who didn't wear jeans or
hippie skirts or smoke marijuana or listen to music with
English lyrics. She didn't care about world order but she
did about domestic order and her private club's social
events. Looking at her, I couldn't help but be surprised

by how different she was from my mom, who, in the words of my dad, was incapable of accomplishing more than one task per day, like grocery shopping and organizing her papers, who always burned the casserole, left the sheets in the washer to mold, and the keys in the door. In short, a disaster. But an incredibly tender disaster to which I was of course deeply attached. The few family reunions I'm able to remember always took place at Aunt Claudine's house. According to Mom, they didn't want to come to our studio because it disgusted them. When I came to their home my aunt and uncle received me with a mix of pity about the situation with my parents and apprehension about the way in which I'd been raised.

My aunt was a practical woman, and to make her life easier decided to have me switch schools that year. Instead of continuing to go to the elementary school in my neighborhood, I'd go to the American School with my cousins. My new school, like my new life, was divided into levels. The majority of the blond students, such as my cousins, studied in the American section of the school. I went to the dingier, Mexican part of the school where they spoke Spanish, whose classrooms were located not on the roof terrace but on the first floor—that is, in the darkest part of the building. Every morning on the school bus my cousins would sit in the back seat and kill time by picking on my classmates.

It's true what my aunt Claudine told my father over the phone a few months later; I made no attempt to integrate. I could have contributed more to family conversations and gone more often to the Sunday cookouts attended by the other relatives who were also my own; I could have asked to join the club where the boys spent Saturday mornings. I could have made a friend, not of both of my cousins, but at least of one of them. Could have bothered to figure out which was the less unfriendly of the two. Instead, I remained almost always a recluse in my room, my eyes fixed on the cracks in the ceiling and my ears alert to the gossip the maid would tell her mother about her employers.

My room, halfway between the servant caste and the family members, perfectly represented my place in that realm. Though it was never said out loud, at dinnertime I could sense a general disapproval of my table manners. My aunt was always criticizing my cousins, the younger one especially, for talking with their mouths full and having their elbows on the table. To me, however, she didn't say a word, and that only increased the animosity I felt from them. It was the main reason I began eating at different times. When I got home from school I'd go up to my room to do my homework and go down to the kitchen just as Isabel was about to put the leftovers in the fridge. I'd also wait until the dining room was empty before coming down, even though sometimes it wasn't so easy resisting the aromas of food wafting up to the terrace. When they had all gone, I'd turn on the lights and make myself a sandwich and drink the hot chocolate Isabel would leave by the stove for me. I ate alone, like a ghost whose life unfolds alongside the living but is uninterrupted by them. I liked the silence and stillness of those moments. Now and again, as I slurped down my chocolate, I would find some trace of Isabel—a grocery list, a pamphlet from the Evangelical church, a soap opera digest. It was funny to see the papers, the girl's clumsy handwriting, her orthographic indecision. After eating I'd wash my plate and utensils and go up to the maid's bathroom which Isabel and her mother would leave full of steam and smelling of Nivea cream.

On Saturdays, while my cousins played tennis at the club, I'd go to the La Merced market with Isabel to do the shopping for the week. We'd take the bus that stopped a few blocks from the house and then another that took us down Vértiz Avenue. The market at La Merced was far more interesting than the little grocery on the same street as my parents' studio, where I used to shop. What I most enjoyed about those outings with Isabel was riding the bus through the city and the characters who rode with us. People of every age and social class, all bumping around and into one another. Also different kinds of beggars, from crippled children to housewives with a venerable air about them. One time I even got to see a clown commit armed robbery; he threatened the driver while we all put our money into his accomplice's bag. Isabel also liked doing the shopping. As soon as she left the house her spirits would lift and she'd talk with me about the things we saw. She'd haggle with the vendors with that same effective cheerfulness.

Of all the lives lived in that house, Clemencia's was undoubtedly the most guarded. More so even than mine. She spoke to no one, avoided the members of the family, and if by chance she ran into one of my cousins on the back staircase, she wouldn't say a word to him. Only at night could she be heard whispering with her daughter in their room. There were times, though, especially if she saw that I was sad or anxious, pacing the terrace as was my custom, when she'd offer me one of the cigarettes she smoked, unbeknownst to Isabel, a few feet away from the gas tanks. I never accepted but would remain by her side while she smoked. The smell of her unfiltered Delicados reminded me of my parents' studio.

I don't know if it was Isabel's exquisite seasoning, the abundance of goodies in the kitchen, or that the sporadic snacking just wasn't enough for me, but at my aunt's house I became a food fanatic. It wasn't only once in a while that I'd leave my room to get food, but several times a night I'd go down for a Coke, a packet of cookies, a yogurt with fruit. It didn't matter how late it was. I remember perfectly how free I felt, to be moving about that house unseen, unheard, and I suspect that from those days came my habit of walking flush to the wall that I mentioned earlier.

In one of these early morning hours in which I'd go downstairs to pour myself a glass of milk I discovered a cockroach, dark brown in color, at a standstill in front of the cupboard. It was like that insect was looking at me, and in its eyes I recognized the same surprise and suspicion that I felt toward it. Then it began running around helter-skelter. Its nervousness disgusted me, and yet, it also felt familiar. Or was it the feeling of familiarity that repulsed me? I can't say. What I do know is that I left my glass on the table and ran terrified to my bedroom. But I couldn't sleep. There were two things on my mind: my cowardly behavior at the sight of a miserable bug and the glass of milk that I'd left on the table. After thinking about it for some time I mustered enough courage to go back downstairs. I found the insect still on the floor. This time it wasn't fear I felt, but an unbounded loathing. I lifted my foot and with the bottom of my sandal stamped it into the tile. The impact produced a crunch that sounded deafening in the dead silence. I started to head back upstairs when I heard the appalled voice of Clemencia, a few feet away.

"If you don't pick her up and get rid of her," she said to me, "her relatives will come looking for her."

The old woman gracefully bent down and picked up the corpse in her hand and wrapped it in a napkin. There was a certain solemnity about her, as if she were performing a funeral rite. She then opened the back door to the patio we shared with neighboring houses and placed it in a potted plant.

We went up to our rooms in silence. Once on the terrace, Clemencia began her lamentations.

"What got into you?" she said, as if to herself. "They will probably invade us now."

I lay in bed for hours, turning it over in my mind. Even to an eleven-year-old, what Clemencia had said sounded a little absurd. In my insomnia I wondered what would happen if Clemencia were right and, if so, what were family ties between cockroaches like? What obligations and rights did they have within their clan? And this family, was it just one, interminable family that inhabited the whole earth, or were there distinctions between the different branches? When at last I fell asleep I dreamt of a funeral procession of cockroaches. The one I had flattened with my foot was lying amidst a throng, like a fallen hero or beloved poet. I felt certain they would never forgive me.

Clemencia was not wrong. Shortly thereafter, cockroaches invaded my aunt Claudine's house. They didn't all come at once, like hordes of Vikings ready to conquer the land. But like guerrillas avoiding detection, surreptitiously they took over the cupboard. Then the entire kitchen. A few days later Isabel called her employer in to tell her the news. I found myself near them just at that moment, and so I saw my speechless aunt's severe and commanding frown. I couldn't get it out of my head that the invasion was my fault. I thought she was going to fire Isabel, but instead, when at last she decided to say something, it was to establish a plan of attack. It would begin with the lowest-grade poison. If that didn't work within seventy-two hours they would call the exterminator. Isabel nodded gravely. Her legs were close together and her back was straight, like a soldier's. Before she left, Claudine paused in the doorway and asked the maid to make her lime blossom tea and bring it to her in bed.

"Don't tell anybody," she said. "This is to stay between us."

But my aunt did not stick to the original plan. Whether it was because she was too proud or too ashamed in front of the neighbors, the exterminator never came to the house. Instead, in the following weeks we saw a rotation of all kinds of traps and poisons meant to mitigate the plague. The most impressive was a type of glue that a few cockroaches got stuck in and left behind a shell, or sometimes just a leg. Unfortunately, the trap didn't kill them. Nor did it sterilize them. Even mutilated those insects continued reproducing rapidly, populating the cupboards and the shelves where the spices were kept. My aunt was the strategist and Isabel the executer. For the latter, the affair with the cockroaches was a personal matter, the long-awaited opportunity for her to prove her loyalty to the family. The sympathy Isabel inspired in me made of me an accomplice in her war. Every night I helped her sprinkle the corners of the house with an odorless white product that supposedly drove away the insects. However, the only result from this new substance was the death of a mouse whose existence meant nothing to us. My aunt Claudine on the other hand preferred aerosol. When neither her sons nor her husband were home she'd appear in the hallways with a face-mask and a can, her formidable bearing reminiscent of a soldier carrying heavy firearms. I could hear the sound of the aerosol from my room and it made me shiver. Isabel and my aunt spoke of nothing else. It was like the insects' presence consumed them. In contrast, my cousins never brought it up. More than once

I wondered if Claudine remained firm in her resolve to keep them out of it or if they themselves preferred to fake dementia. I suspect they knew about it, but fearful of their mother's nerves or maybe just indifferent, they decided to play dumb and not say anything about it. Until my aunt brought it out into the open in order to step up preventative measures.

"It's important," Claudine said to all us, "to be extra careful with food. Dirty plates must not be left in the living room or TV room. I don't want to see a single crumb on the floor."

My cousins earnestly adopted all the hygienic measures their mother imposed. So did I, becoming a stranger to myself. Before, when I saw a spider or Jerusalem cricket in the playground at school, my reaction had always been calm and unconcerned. And now I considered those bugs a matter of life and death. The zeal quickly rubbed off on my cousins. Every time a cockroach appeared in the bathroom or on someone's pillow, the entire family came to pester it, Isabel and me included. It was no longer a question of social class but a full-on war between species. Those insects had invaded not only the drawers and cupboards, but also the cracks in our mind. Anyone who has suffered them knows I'm not exaggerating when I say that ultimately, cockroaches almost always become an obsession.

Clemencia was the only one who stayed out of the whole affair. Her behavior seemed strange to me, especially after her outburst that first night. I was sure that she knew many things about our enemies, and yet she revealed nothing. She would only speak sarcastically, once in a while, about our aggressiveness:

"That's the rich for you," she'd say. "Agonizing over the littlest thing. Look at them, you'd think the blight was upon them."

She was forgetting that her own daughter was one of those leading the attack on the insects.

According to what she'd said that night, cockroaches have codes and rituals, at least around death. I told myself that it was crucial to observe their behavior more systematically, and that from such observation the keys to how to annihilate them would become apparent.

The enemy seemed unfazed by our attacks. The cockroaches walked around the house so defiantly it seemed like arrogance. Maybe it was because they were, at least in numbers, superior to us or maybe because death to them, unlike to humans, means nothing. It was this characteristic, and not the color of their shells or the hideousness of their nervous legs, that most terrified me. Of one thing I was certain: if we didn't exile them, they would us.

One Saturday morning Isabel and I sat in the kitchen talking. We had put bread in the microwave to thaw. As the woman was explaining to me the benefits of the new insecticide, we heard an unusual crackling coming from the appliance. When we opened the door we found three cockroach corpses on our snack. Evidently, the top of the microwave (which we rarely used) was one of their main headquarters. The scene horrified me; we had tried everything, and nothing had worked. In contrast, Isabel remained strangely calm.

"Don't worry," she said to me protectively. "We're going to win this war . . ."

Isabel stopped using insecticide that week. Never losing for an instant her newfound calmness, she began hunting down the bugs and putting them in an empty yogurt jar. The following Saturday my aunt went with us to La Merced, driving her car rather than taking the bus. We did the shopping like always but this time, before leaving, Isabel led us to a section she'd never taken me to before. The stalls there didn't have metal curtains or display tables like they did in other zones. There, the vendors laid out their wares on the ground. A sheet or a mat was enough to display their goods. Some had herbs, others, little piles of wild berries, loquats, and plums they had clearly gathered themselves. Others sold baskets. Someone at one of those miserable stalls caught my attention. It was a little girl with a lovely and very dark face who was helping her mother sell insects.

"What are they selling?" I asked Isabel in disbelief.

"Jumiles," responded the little girl in a voice so sweet I instantly blushed. "Want to try?"

I looked at the scene, astonished. The girl was selling round and very squirmy insects in paper cones, and the customers were eating them, there on the spot, with lime and salt and not even bothering to cook them first.

"What are you waiting for? Go on," Isabel chided me as my aunt watched, amused. "You're going to say no to that angel? She's giving them to you!"

I extended my hand and in it the girl placed one of

those little cups, overflowing with jumiles. She dressed them for me herself.

Despite everything my aunt could say about my parents' eccentricities, I'd never eaten insects before. Not even grasshoppers. As I deliberated whether to try them, one of the critters escaped and started crawling up my forearm. I couldn't take it; I threw the cone on the ground and took off running. Isabel found me at the gate that separated that section from the next one, where they sold fruit and where we always went.

Jumiles were not the only bugs they sold there. There were also vendors who sold bees, whose venom—I learned that morning—helps reduce inflammation in wounds and lower fevers, brown crickets, corn earworms, ahuatles, and some enormous ants they called *chicatanas*. According to the institution at the university where I work, the number of known edible insects in Mexico is approaching 507 species.

"See? There's nothing wrong with eating insects," Isabel said to my aunt, who continued regarding her with a pensive expression. "I swear to you, señora. If we start eating them, the cockroaches will flee in terror."

"But how are we supposed to convince my husband and the boys to go along with it?" Claudine asked to my surprise.

"We won't tell them at first. We'll just serve them, and once they get used to it, we'll explain everything. Or we can bring them here and they'll figure it out."

On Monday when I came home from school I saw that my aunt had been convinced. For dinner Isabel served a salad of lettuce and breaded, fried fish. For dressing she brought out several spicy sauces, salt, and slices of lime. From the kitchen I watched as my family devoured that new dish with their usual appetite. My aunt also ate it, but not as much and somewhat reluctantly, with the expression of a martyr absorbed in her sacrifice. I didn't eat a bite. The next day they had chop-suey and on Wednesday different kinds of mushrooms in guajillo chili sauce. That whole week Isabel kept coming up with delicious dishes. After a few days and for no apparent reason, the cockroach population in our cupboard had diminished. My aunt was overjoyed and called her sons over to explain to them what was going on.

"Don't tell your father yet," she advised. "I don't think he's ready."

My cousins seemed upset at first. The younger one threw up that evening and refused to eat for several days. However, soon enough we all got over our prejudices and began to enjoy our supremacy over the cockroaches immensely. So great was the animosity we felt toward them that we'd think up all kinds of ways to torture them. The family's favorite recipe was cockroach ceviche, which Isabel would prepare in front of everybody. To make it she'd dry the wretched things using fragrant herbs, as you would grasshoppers, and once purged, she'd leave them to marinate in lime juice for a few hours. I now know that many people develop allergies to cockroaches. Just the insects' presence will make their eyes puffy and watery. However, maybe because of the highly scrupulous way Isabel cooked the cockroaches, nobody in the family developed that kind of reaction. Ingesting the cockroaches not only helped us end the plague, it also fostered a kinship among us. I began eating with the family again, being careful with my manners, and my cousins stopped segregating me for my ill breeding. Nothing like a family secret to strengthen the unity between its members.

Clemencia alone did not participate in these feasts. If before she had kept to herself, now her gastronomic reticence marginalized her completely. One night I was awakened by a whispered conversation. Isabel and her mother were having a heated discussion in their room. I put on my sandals and went out to listen through the door.

"It may be the solution, but you don't have the right. It's not fair what you're doing," said the old woman on the verge of tears.

I knew Clemencia well enough to know that she didn't give a damn what the habitants of the house ate. I couldn't believe it; she was defending the cockroaches. But Isabel, who somehow hadn't realized whose side her mother was on, kept insisting, over and over, that it was the only way to defeat them. I once saw a program on TV about how insects get rid of each other. The best way to finish off a species is to let another one eat it. Isabel was right and the results spoke for themselves.

Days later, as I kept her company while she smoked one of her unfiltered Delicados, Clemencia spoke to me about the cockroaches, with obvious admiration.

"Those animals were the first inhabitants of Earth

and even if the world were to end tomorrow, they would survive. They are the memory of our ancestors. They are our grandparents and our descendants. Do you realize what it means to eat them?"

Clemencia was not joking with that question. The kinship seemed invaluable to her. I told her that Isabel and I weren't trying to exterminate the entire species, we just wanted them out of the house.

"Besides there's nothing wrong with eating insects!" I exclaimed, using Isabel's words. "They sell them in the market."

Clemencia remained silent, and as she did she looked at me, accusingly and full of resentment. "Nobody, except for you people, eats cockroaches. But in this life we must pay for all we do. Don't be surprised by your bad luck."

I returned to my room terrified by the old woman's threat. I'd already seen how her crazy predictions come true.

Friday morning my aunt came to school to bring me home. I asked her if something bad had happened but she only shook her head no. She looked so serious that I didn't dare ask anything else. We rode the entire way in silence. In the foyer I recognized my mother's coat. From the living room came the diffused, peculiar scent of her dark cigarettes. I was surprised by how outdated her clothes looked. In the months I'd spent in that housing complex I had gotten used to the sheen of middle-class clothing and spotless furniture.

Much skinnier than before, my mother was perched

on the arm of the couch and shaky with nerves. Breaking the rules of the house—rules she knew perfectly well—she lit cigarette after cigarette and inhaled deeply, as if in the drifting substance entering her lungs she hoped to find the courage to look me in the eyes. She hadn't come for me. She seemed more interested to know if I was well behaved, if I did my homework and my chores, and if my aunt would agree to let me stay longer. Some comment was made about a bank account that would take care of her expenses, or mine. I didn't really understand that part. What I did easily grasp was that she was very frightened. Practical as ever, my aunt gave me the explanation her sister was not able to formulate:

"Your mother has decided to check herself into a clinic. We think it's best and we are supporting her."

Before I could answer, Claudine left the room so we'd be alone. Mom trembled in silence. I went over to the couch and with all the affection in the world hugged her. All of my doubts disappeared in that moment; as accustomed as I'd become to the new family, I still belonged to her and it was with her that I wanted to live. In a low voice, a voice for secrets, I told her about my cousins, about how horrible riding the bus with them was; I exaggerated as much as I could my living conditions so that she would take me with her to the studio, to the clinic, to wherever. I promised to take care of her and in response I received the heat of her tarred breath. After a few minutes my aunt returned to take her away.

I remember the heavy downpour that fell that night. Isabel and Clemencia knocked on my door several times. The silhouette of the umbrella reflected in one of my windows. It's not that I didn't want to see or speak to them. I just didn't have the strength to get out of bed and open the door. The only company I had was that of a very small cockroach who remained near the desk in the corner all night. An orphaned cockroach, probably frightened, who didn't know which way to turn.

Felina

The ties between animals and human beings can be as complex as those that bind us people. There are some who maintain bonds of reluctant cordiality with their pets. They feed them, they take them for walks if need be, but rarely do they speak to them other than to scold or "educate" them. In contrast, there are others who make of their turtles their closest confidants. Every night they lean in toward their tanks and tell them about what happened to them at work, the confrontation they put off with their boss, their doubts, and their hopes for love. Among domestic animals dogs get particularly good press. It is even said that they are man's best friend because of their loyalty and nobility, words that often signify nothing more than a tolerance for abuse and abandonment. Dogs are generally good animals, true. But I've also heard about some who don't recognize their masters and, fed up or in a fit of madness, attack them, causing the same bewildered reaction as when a mother hits her young children. Felines on the other hand suffer a reputation of being selfish and overly independent. I don't at all share this opinion. It's true that cats are less demanding than dogs and their presence often much less imposing, at times barely even noticeable. However, I know from experience that they can come to develop enormous empathy toward others of their species, as well as toward their owners. In reality, cats are highly versatile animals and their natures range from the ostracism of a turtle to the omnipresence of a dog.

My understanding of cats goes back to when I was still in college. I was finishing a degree in history and my dream was to do my postgraduate work abroad, at a prestigious university if possible. In those days I was renting a spacious and sunny apartment I occasionally shared with other students and then later on with two cats. Now that I think about it, roommates can some-times fill the role of pets and ties with them are just as complex. Two men and one woman lived with me in that apartment. The first studied architecture but was passionate about tattoos. He decorated his room with colorful posters of naked Japanese men and almost never opened his curtains. The woman was more social. She liked to invite friends over and organize movie mara-thons with them. However, she was a closet bulimic, which made splitting the cost of groceries unfair and an issue she refused to discuss with me. The day I felt obligated to say something she decided to move out. The third tenant, a man with a much more low-key personality, was studying to be a doctor and spent a lot of time at the hospital. As he was never around, he was by far the best. He stayed just over six months, and then left the city to complete his residency.

The cats, unlike the roommates, provided genuine and stable company. When I was a child several animals passed through my parents' house: a rabbit, a German Shepherd, a hamster, and two European house cats who never met each other. While I considered the pets of my childhood to be mine, they were never my responsibility. All I had to do was enjoy them; their care was in the hands of my parents. But the cats I had as a student depended entirely on me. From the moment they entered my life I felt I had to protect them, and it was that feeling, completely new to me, that made me adopt them.

They appeared one unusually cold morning in December. Marisa, my thesis advisor and someone who was becoming a friend, called to tell me she had found them in a plastic bag in the street, tied together by someone who obviously wanted them dead. They were kittens still too young to be weaned. I was so moved by the story that I said I would take them and immediately went to pick them up. My compassion toward them grew when I opened the box and saw them, voicelessly mewing and still trembling from going so long without oxygen.

"Keep a close eye on them," my advisor recommended. "They may have suffered lesions on their brains. It wouldn't hurt to bring them to a vet."

That's what I did. I took them to the clinic she recommended and there I learned their approximate age and sex. They were a male and a female. He, black like a bad omen with little white markings between his nose and whiskers; she, striped, a bit reddish, rather small in frame and thin. A poet and an actress, I thought. I decided to call them Milton and Greta. Months later, when they'd recovered and began to reveal their true personalities, I'd find that the names couldn't have suited them better; the male displayed a sullen disposition, but also an incredible generosity; and the female, the attitude of a diva fully aware of her beauty. I barely got to see them in the first days after I brought them home. As soon as we arrived and I took them out of the box they ran and hid behind the refrigerator. The sound, I imagine, reminded them of their mother's purr. Instead of trying to force contact upon them, I'd leave them plates of food and milk so that they could eat when they were alone and felt safe.

After two weeks the cats had not only come out of hiding, they had taken over the apartment. It had been a few months since I'd shared the apartment with anyone and the company of those two kittens felt wonderful. I watched them from my desk in a corner in the living room as they leapt about on the furniture, sprang onto the coffee and dining tables with surprising agility, and rested peacefully on the floor beneath a sunbeam. Milton liked to be near me when I worked. He'd snuggle against my feet and fall asleep as I typed. Greta, however, preferred that I paid attention to nothing but her, with long, slow caresses. She'd mew for them every time I came home from some outing to the library or movies.

Though I had several friends I'd see from time to time, at parties or public events for my department, that year I led a rather solitary existence, obsessed with writing my thesis to which I dedicated most of my time. I didn't have a partner. For the first three years of the program I'd been in a stable relationship with another student in the department and I didn't like any of those I'd met since well enough to sleep with them more than once or twice, more out of loneliness than anything else and always in an intoxicated state and late at night. The cats eased considerably that need for affection. The three of us were a team. I contributed a quiet and maternal energy; Greta, liveliness and coquetry; and Milton, masculine vigor. So pleasant was the equilibrium we established between us that I thought a long while before choosing a roommate with whom to split the utility bills. I still interviewed possible new candidates as they turned up but I didn't accept any of them, for fear the intruder would disrupt the atmosphere in the house. The cats did not look kindly on having a fourth person, either. Aware—god knows how—of my intentions, they were visibly hostile toward the candidates. If a girl, Greta would bare her fangs and raise every hair on her body. If on the other hand the candidate was a guy, Milton would shame-lessly mark his territory by urinating on the interested student's shoes. Thankfully, the scholarship I had at the time was enough to cover the bills.

Animals develop more quickly than human beings. In the year I spent with the cats I remained practically the same. They, however, changed remarkably. From two scrawny and skittish kittens they turned into teen-agers, and then into young adults at the height of their beauty. Hormones began to dominate them as did mine during my period. Milton felt compelled to urinate in the corners and on the houseplants, and the first time Greta went into heat she did so with very little dis-cretion, mewing in high-pitched, frenzied tones, lifting her tail and rubbing her vulva against every furniture edge she could find. It was shocking to see her that way, and I felt sorry for her. The unfulfillment of her desire was as overwhelming as its intensity. Unlike my periods, which lasted about five days, Greta's seemed to never end. If I was sensitive to her condition, Milton was especially so. He'd circle her, constantly pursue her and try to mount her, to ease once and for all so much frustration. But Greta cruelly rejected his advances and we all suffered for it. Cultures that believe in reincar-nation almost always consider it a reward to be born among the male ranks and a disadvantage to reincarnate into the female. Seeing Greta, normally so composed, so overpowered by reproductive hormones made me think that this seemingly misogynistic and primitive theory might not be so absurd. It was then I decided to take my cat to the vet. I wanted to see if it was possible to give her some relief and maybe a contraceptive, so she could go roam the neighborhood rooftops as she pleased. However, what the doctor suggested as a solution for all the evils and dangers my pet faced seemed to me excessively cruel. According to him, the best thing to do was cut out her ovaries, without delay, before she was full grown.

"And leave her sterile forever?" I asked, horrified. "That's why you became a vet?"

The man remained in guilty silence as I looked at my cat, defenseless on the table. I told myself that neither one of us could choose for her; she had the right to be a mother, at least one time. What other mission was there in animal life, I asked myself, but reproduction? To take away her ovaries was to deny her the chance to fulfill it.

Furious, I walked out of the clinic without explanation. As I was about to get into the taxi the vet appeared in the doorway and shouted:

"Keep her inside, at least for this month. She's too young for a successful pregnancy."

I returned to the apartment with the incandescent Greta in her cage. I was not about to let anyone but nature decide her fate and that of her descendants.

Around that time there was a new roommate applicant. A Basque anthropology student who had come to spend three weeks in the city doing his fieldwork. Strangely, neither of the cats—still disturbed by Greta's overexcitement, I guess—was hostile toward him on the afternoon I had him come by to see the apartment. I figured that three weeks bore no threat to our cohabitation and would bring in extra money in perfect timing with the vacation that was around the corner. And so the next day the Basque moved into the free bedroom. Ander, as he was named, was a boy with a full beard and blue eyes. He was rather shy and didn't call much attention to himself and spent most of his time studying at the Central Library. During the few hours he spent at home he was polite, helpful even, and from time to time, in our brief conversations, he'd reveal a strange and therefore interesting sense of humor. I remember the night he came home while I was still working and told me he had bought a laughable amount of marijuana for an exorbitant price. In this country, as in so many others, there is the custom of taking advantage of foreigners as much as possible. I felt embarrassed when I heard his account and as recompense offered him two joints I'd had for several months. He cheered up and, extremely appreciative, invited me to smoke on his balcony. Under the effect of cannabis my roommate's sense of humor emerged uninhibited. After the first three hits he started telling me jokes about the Basques, which cracked me up. We then talked about Mexico and its idiosyncrasies, the apartment, the cats, Greta's inexorable desire. We exhausted every anecdote, laughing at the poor cat in heat. It was perhaps in her honor that we ended up thrashing about on the mattress I kept for roommates. We had a good time, but it was the only time. In the three weeks of his stay we shared the utilities, groceries, and my stash of weed, but never again a bed.

Rather than suffering because of Ander's absence, I accepted it placidly and with an unsettling serenity. Greta's period had ended a few days earlier, and with it the crazed mewing. I finished my thesis by the deadline and turned it in to my advisor for final corrections. I also applied to several graduate programs in history at universities abroad and started planning a vacation I'd spend on some beach on the Pacific coast while waiting for my professional exam. It was around that time I began noticing evident changes in my cat's body, changes I might have noticed earlier had I not been so busy.

She wasn't as agile when leaping; her previously tiny nipples gained volume and her torso considerable girth. The news of her pregnancy made me happy for her, but also a little worried because of the vet's warning. Still, enthusiasm won out. In probably just a few months I'd have an apartment full of playful kittens. I emptied out my bottom dresser drawer and carefully prepared a soft place for them. Greta was meeker and more affectionate toward me than ever, and gratefully accepted my petting and attention. But the happiness was short lived. Fifteen days after Ander left my period didn't come when it should have and didn't come late, as I naïvely expected it to. I took a home pregnancy test and prayed, as I was sitting on the toilet, for it to be negative. However, two lines stained the white oval, confirming my fears. In the passing of a few minutes the happy and tender mind-set Greta's pregnancy had put me in turned into a nightmare. I didn't have the faintest idea what I should do, not even what I really wanted.

I was in a state of shock for a week, wondering if I should seek advice or decide on my own, if it was wise to tell Ander—with whom I'd hardly had any contact in the past few weeks—wondering, above all, if I wanted and was able to take on motherhood at that point in my life. If I did, my child would probably grow up without a father. That Ander was a foreigner, a fact I'd initially been grateful for and that had encouraged as much closeness as it did distance, now complicated things even more. I barely knew him. I couldn't even really say what kind of person he was. But then, what kind of person was I? The answers that came to mind were not that flattering. I'd always had a hard time making decisions. It was hard for me even with trivial matters to discard many options in favor of one, and in that moment this very annoying characteristic took on disproportionate dimensions. As I watched Greta dragging her cumbersome body across the hardwood floor, I got a taste of the many forms of helplessness. Like hers, my body was changing with dizzying speed. The fatigue, and especially the nausea, made any activity beyond the most essential—showering, grocery shopping, feeding the cats—an impossible feat. The rest of my time was spent in bed, in the company of Milton, who never stopped purring in my ear. Those were very confusing days.

Every time my mind seemed to finally clear and reveal some hint of a decision, the impulse was crushed by an immense guilt.

One morning an envelope with Princeton letterhead appeared, earlier than I'd imagined it would, beneath my door. Opening the letter I found that not only had I been accepted, I was being considered for a really good grant. Instead of making me happy, the news increased the weight pressing on my shoulders. I quickly got dressed and brought the letter to my advisor's cubicle to show her. Marisa was surprised by my appearance.

"Look at those bags under your eyes," she said, laughing. "You received a letter from Princeton, not a death sentence."

I told her what was going on. She listened to my reasoning and sobbing without saying a word and, once I'd stopped talking, recommended that I take all the time I needed before deciding what to do.

"Move forward with the formal procedure, take care of the requirements, and maybe things will be more clear as the date approaches. It's no easy thing to make this kind of decision," she added respectfully, though I knew perfectly well what deep down she expected me to do. Before I left her office she handed me a piece of paper with her gynecologist's information.

"Should you decide, call his cell phone and tell him I sent you."

After that everything sped up. If in the previous two weeks Greta and I were on the same lethargic rhythm, going from the bed to the couch and back, from then on we began to move around in different directions at different speeds. While Greta walked cautiously and ran to hide every time the phone or doorbell rang, enjoying her pregnancy and the intoxicating effect of the hormones, I battled with my own symptoms, investing all my energy in collecting signatures and visiting professors who could help me. I'd make Greta a rich meal and then as soon as I walked out of the kitchen I'd search the Internet for articles and all the information I could find on abortion, which was still illegal in that city in those days. I read testimonials, I researched the different ways to perform one, from the morning-after pill—not a viable option at my late stage—to homemade teas, suction, scraping.

One afternoon I mustered the courage to call my advisor's gynecologist. I explained the situation and asked for an appointment. The doctor was very kind and saw me that same day, fitting me in between patients. I remember that his office was on the fourteenth floor of a skyscraper that didn't have a thirteenth floor. Everything was white and obsessively antiseptic. The relaxing melody of the background music only worsened my nerves. It was a struggle to wait my turn and not run into the street, but I managed. Once inside I let the nurse put me through the routine exam: height, weight, blood pressure. Afterward the doctor I'd spoken to on the phone came in. A man of about fifty who reminded me, god knows why—maybe for the white coat or because my advisor had recommended him as well—of Greta's veterinarian. With a smile on his lips and that paternal sweetness those in his profession often possess, he explained the procedure to me. And at the end he added:

"You have to come on an empty stomach and with someone who can take you back to your house. Even though I don't use general anesthesia, you'll be drowsy and weak."

As I listened to him I thought of Greta, who at that time must have been lying on the armchair in the living room, soaking up the afternoon sun. I wordlessly nodded a few times, including when the gynecologist took out his appointment book and suggested a date for the procedure. I paid for the visit and went out to face the most desolate evening of my entire life, an evening of sweltering heat, and no matter where I was it was hard to breathe.

When I got home, Greta was there at the door, expecting her normal session of cuddling. This time she let me rub her belly, already considerably swollen. As I did I asked myself if I also had some mission in life. I didn't come up with an answer.

That night I tried calling my advisor to tell her about the visit to her doctor and that, despite his friendless and general kind disposition, I had decided to forgo his services. I would not be going to Princeton. I also decided not to go forward with the paperwork for the grant or worry about anything besides my pregnancy. Later, maybe in September, I'd start working on a doctorate. But here, at the same university in which I was currently enrolled. However, that night Marisa's phone rang again and again with no answer. I had no choice but to leave a message asking her to call me back.

On Friday Greta woke up a little sick. Her eyes were sad and her ears flat. She curled up in the drawer I'd prepared for her kittens and didn't move from there except to use the litter box. I did the math: it was still about three weeks until she was due, so that couldn't have been the reason for her lack of energy. She wasn't better by evening so I decided to bring her to the vet. I hadn't done so earlier out of disdain for the man I could see as nothing but an animal sterilizer. It was past six o'clock. The vet was going to close in forty minutes so I called a taxi and put Greta in her cage as fast as possible. It was essentially a fool's errand; the place was a few miles from my apartment and anyone who knows Friday rush-hour traffic in this deranged city would have given up. But I needed to know that Greta was all right. I grabbed her cage, she, mewing the whole time in protest at being taken from the apartment, and ran down the stairs not thinking about the risks, not even about the steps, which were against me that day. I tripped on one of them and bounced on my hips a few times. As I fell, I took Greta's cage in both hands so it wouldn't crash to the ground. It was a scare but the accident had no further consequences. I was fine. Despite my prediction, we made it to the veterinarian just before they closed the clinic. After giving her a physical examination and listening to her heart, the doctor congratulated us both; mother and kittens were doing marvelously. The only thing ailing Greta was an extreme, though normal, exhaustion.

I was in the taxi on my way home when I started to feel the pain in my waist and muscles. Later I learned that in such situations adrenaline acts as an anesthetic and it isn't until the scare is over that you feel the effects of a hard hit. As I got undressed in my bedroom that night I saw I'd started bleeding. I didn't want to wait until the next day to call the doctor. I took advantage of having his cell number and called him to find out how I could save the baby. Marisa's gynecologist seemed worried at first, but he quickly recovered his paternal demeanor and told me, delicately, that it would be difficult to do something. He told me to be patient and come in the next morning for a thorough examination. Some people swear there is no such thing as an accident. I don't fully agree with that. But still, I can't say if my fall that evening was an accident or a Freudian slip. I am sure that it was not at all intentional. A team of scientists I met a few months later at Princeton University claim that if they put all our genetic information, education, and the most significant events in our lives into a computer and give us a hundred different dilemmas and make us choose for each one, the machine would figure out our responses before we could think them. In reality—so they say—we don't make decisions. All of our choices are preconditioned. Anyway, in that instant I didn't get to make a decision, and I don't know if I would have wanted to know what such a computer would say about it.

The next day I went to the doctor's office first thing, neglecting no small number of prior commitments.

The gynecologist examined me as he'd said he would and confirmed the prognosis he'd given me the night before. Nothing could be done.

"You're lucky it happened so early on," he said with an incomprehensible optimism. "We won't have to scrape your uterus to expel the residue."

I left bereaved, as if I hadn't had any doubts about the pregnancy. Rather than improving after that, my mood grew increasingly worse. It seemed like reality was a black hole where there was no room for exciting opportunities to come. My thesis advisor, who was so supportive, assured me more than once that my inconsolable sadness came from a violent change in my hormone production. That could very well be, but knowing it didn't help. At the end of the day, whether I liked it or not, I was also an animal and my body and my mind alike reacted to the loss of my offspring just as Greta's would have had she lost her kittens. It's true that I was no longer as stressed as before, when the course of things was mine to direct, but the buildup of earlier pressures, added to the sadness I felt, submerged me in a state of depression in which it wasn't even possible for me to return to what had been my basic routine. I stopped showering and eating and, of course, thinking of my studies.

From then on Greta was in the habit of always lying in my lap, as if instinctively trying to cover with her body the absence of the baby I used to carry in my womb. It repulsed me. Her purr agitated me, and I'd push her off. But my cat, undeterred, would come lie on me again after a few minutes. It was Marisa who took over my correspondence with Princeton. Had it not been for her, I wouldn't have been accepted, let alone granted a scholarship. More than a thesis advisor or friend, she acted like a mother toward me.

Shortly after that Greta brought into the world six perfectly healthy kittens. I didn't get to witness the birth; I didn't even hear it. It happened early one morning, as I slept with the help of some sleeping pills my advisor had given me. When I woke up I felt a kind of bustling around beneath my sheets and I saw that they'd been born not in the drawer I had so lovingly prepared for them, but in my bed, in the space between my legs. That awed me no end. What kind of reality do animals conceive of, or at least, what kind of reality did my cat conceive of where I was concerned? It's obvious that her gesture was not happenstance but of her own choosing, if it is that cats, unlike we humans, do make certain decisions. The newborns made high-pitched noises, like birds shrieking; they squirmed about constantly, attached to their mother who lay there stretched out before them, allowing the six to feed from her nipples. It was Greta, much more than those barely formed creatures, who awoke in me an immense tenderness. Her surrender to her kittens' sucking was total, and at the same time, she could not have looked more exultant. I spent a moment in silence with her, watching her in her role as proud mother, as if, rather than an instinct, her manner and her attentiveness spoke to a sacrifice, its results now visible.

I carefully got out of bed, and as I was making breakfast, I realized that for the first time in two weeks I didn't want not to exist. I called Marisa after to tell her the good news. When I went back into the bedroom, neither Greta nor her kittens were on the bed. I imagined her carrying them one by one by their necks to the dresser drawer, where Milton, responsible I suppose for fathering the litter, had also made himself comfortable. Everything seemed to be in its place. In those days the only thing that brought me any real joy was seeing Greta with her children. When she wasn't nursing them she was cleaning them with her tongue, licking them day and night, one at a time, with admirable dedication. If she left them a moment alone in the drawer, it was to eat or to use the litter box. The rest of the time she dwelled in absolute and blissful devotion.

Little by little I regained my enthusiasm for my studies and for my upcoming trip. That year I didn't go on some beach vacation. Instead I focused on preparing for the professional exam and packing all of my belongings into boxes. Cautiously at first, so as not to disturb the young family. Then more boldly as it got closer to my due date. Knowing what Milton and Greta meant to me, Marisa offered to take them. And when Greta's brood was old enough, she'd find them good homes. She had a huge house with a garden, and promised me they'd be no trouble.

"Just the opposite. They'll fill the void from your leaving."

I knew the cats couldn't be in better hands. But still, I promised her it would just be for a little while as I got settled in Princeton.

The day of the professional exam came and I was confident as I took it. My grades were as high as we'd expected. I told my landlady I'd be leaving the apartment. Once all my books were boxed up I started to pack my bags and either store or give away the clothing I wasn't bringing. People came and went from my apartment, buying or taking things, loaded down with bags of books or cookware. The move was taking over the apartment with an increasingly frenetic rhythm, like a phenomenon with a will of its own. Greta's kittens ran all over the place, climbing on the boxes, the stacks of books, and the living room furniture. The only thing that remained in its place was the dresser drawer, soft and cozy, like the last bastion of an epoch coming to a close, in which I often wanted to hide. In there, where the eight of them slept increasingly cramped together, nobody seemed fazed by the change. But it only seemed that way. Marisa and I had decided that she'd come for the cats two days before I left and one day before the moving truck came for the furniture. I don't really remember if we'd spoken in her office or on the phone. But one thing is for certain; the cats understood.

The evening before, when I came home after an exhausting day of higher-education bureaucracy, I noticed that the cats weren't there. I searched the whole apartment for them and I looked for a way they could have escaped from it. The only thing I was able to determine was that the balcony door was open. I cannot describe the grief I felt. We hadn't even had the chance to say goodbye. "Cats do decide," I remember thinking. I felt like a fool for not having realized it.

Fungus

When I was a little girl my mother had a fungus on one of her toenails. On her left pinkie toe to be exact. From the moment she discovered it she tried everything to get rid of it. Every morning she'd step out of the shower and with the help of a tiny brush pour over her toe a capful of iodine whose smell and sepia, almost reddish tone I remember well. She saw to no avail several dermatologists, including the most prestigious and expensive in the city, who repeated the same diagnoses and suggested the same futile treatments, from traditional clotrimazole ointments to apple cider vinegar. The most radical among them even prescribed her a moderate dose of cortisone, which only inflamed my mother's yellowed toe. Despite her efforts to banish it, the fungus remained there for years until a Chinese doctor to whom nobody—not even my mother—gives credit, was able to drive it away in a few days. It happened so unexpectedly that I could not help wondering if the parasite itself hadn't decided to move on to another place.

Until that moment fungi had always been—at least for me—curious mushrooms that appeared in children's book illustrations and that I associated with the forest and elves. In any case, nothing to do with that rugosity that gave my mother's toenail the texture of an oyster shell. However, more than the dubious and shifting appearance, more than its tenacity and attachment to the invaded toe, what I remember best about the whole affair was the disgust and repulsion the parasite inspired in my mother. I have seen other people over the years with mycosis on different parts of their body. All kinds of mycoses, from those that cause the bottom of the foot to dry out and peel to the circular red fungi you often see on chefs' hands. Most people bear them with resignation, some with stoicism, others with genuine disregard. My mother on the other hand suffered the presence of her fungus as if it were a mortifying affliction. Terrified by the thought that it might spread to the rest of her foot, or worse, her entire body, she separated the affected toenail with a thick piece of cotton to keep it from rubbing against the adjacent toe. She never wore sandals and avoided taking off her socks in front of anyone she wasn't very close to. If for some reason she had to use a public shower she always wore plastic slippers, and to swim in a pool she'd take off her shoes right at the edge just before diving in, so that nobody would see her feet. And so much the better; if anyone had found out about that toe and all the treatments it had been through, they would have thought that instead of a simple fungus, what my mother had was the beginning of leprosy.

Children, unlike adults, adapt to everything. So little by little, despite my mother's disgust, I began to see that fungus as an everyday presence in my family life. It didn't inspire the same aversion in me as it did my mother; just the opposite. I felt a protective sympathy for that iodine-painted toenail, which seemed vulnerable to me, similar to what I would have felt for a crippled pet that had trouble moving around. Time went on and my mother stopped making such a fuss over her affliction. For my part, I grew up and completely forgot about it and never again thought about fungi until I met Philippe Laval.

At that time I had just turned thirty-five. I was married to a patient and generous man who was ten years my senior and the director of the National School of Music, where I had completed the first part of my training as a violinist. We didn't have children. We had tried for a while, but rather than agonizing over it, I felt fortunate to be able to focus on my career. I had completed my training at Juilliard and had garnered certain international prestige, enough to be invited to Europe and the United States to give concerts two or three times a year. I'd just recorded a CD in Denmark and was about to return to Copenhagen to teach a six-week course in a palace that every summer hosted the best students in the world.

I remember one Friday afternoon shortly before I was to leave I received a list with the biographical information of all the professors who would be at the residency that year. Laval's was among them. It wasn't the first time I read his name. He was a violinist and conductor of great renown, and on more than one occasion I'd heard from the mouths of friends words of praise about his live performances and how naturally he led the orchestra with his violin. From the list I learned that he was French and lived in Brussels, but often went to Vancouver where he taught at the School of Art. That weekend my husband, Mauricio, had gone out of town to attend a conference. I didn't have plans that night so I searched the Internet to find which of his concerts was available to purchase online. After browsing for a while I ended up buying one of Beethoven, filmed live at Carnegie Hall years earlier. I remember the sense of wonderment I felt listening to it. The night was hot. I had the balcony doors open to let fresh air in and still, emotion restricted my breathing. Every violinist knows that arrangement—many by heart—but hearing his interpretation was an absolute revelation. As if I could at last understand it in all its depth. I felt a mix of reverence, envy, and gratitude. I listened to it three times at least and each time produced the same shiver. I then searched for pieces interpreted by other musicians invited to Copenhagen, and while the level was undoubtedly very high, not one of them surprised me as much as Laval did. Afterward I closed the file and though I thought of him more than once, I didn't listen to the concert again in the following two weeks.

It wasn't the first time I'd be separated from Mauricio for a few months, but being accustomed to it didn't lessen the sadness of leaving him. As I did for every long trip, I asked him to come with me. The residency allowed it and despite his insisting otherwise I'm sure his work did as well. He could at least have spent two of the six weeks of the course there, or visited me once at the beginning and again at the end of my stay. Had he accepted, things between us would have gone down a different path. However, it didn't make sense to him. He said that the time would go by quickly for us both and the best thing for me would be to concentrate on my work. It would be, according to him, an incredible opportunity, one I couldn't miss or cut short, to plumb my depths and collaborate with other musicians. And it was that, just not in the way we'd imagined.

The castle where the summer school was held was located in Christiania, a neighborhood just outside the city. It was late July and at night the temperature was very pleasant. I wasted almost no time in making friends with Laval. At the beginning his schedule was more or less the same as mine: he was unquestionably nocturnal; I was still on North American time. After classes we'd work the same hours in soundproof rooms so as not to wake the others, and now and again we'd run into each other in the kitchen or at the tea stand. We were the first—and only—ones to make it to the early breakfast, when the cafeteria began serving. From friendly and excessively polite our conversations became increasingly personal. An intimacy quickly grew between us, and a sense of closeness different from what I felt toward the other teachers.

A summer school is a place beyond reality that allows us to surrender to that which we usually deny ourselves. You can take all kinds of liberties; to visit the heart of the host city, attend dinners and events, socialize with the locals or other residents, give in to laziness, to bulimia, to some addicting habit. Laval and I fell into the temptation of falling in love. A classic, it would seem, in such a place. During the six weeks of the program we passed through Copenhagen's parks on buses and bikes, went to bars and museums, attended operas and several concerts. But mostly we were intent on getting to know each other as much as possible in that limited amount of time. When you know a relationship is fated to end on a given day it is easy to let fall the walls you put up to protect yourself. We are more benign, more indulgent with someone who will soon cease to be there than with those who take shape as long-term partners. No fault, no defect deters us, as we won't have to stand it in the future. When a relationship has an expiration date as clear as ours had, there's no wasting time on judging the other person. The only thing you focus on is enjoying their best qualities, fully, urgently, voraciously, as time is not on your side. At least that is what happened to Philippe and me during that residency. His infinite quirks when it came to work, to sleep, and to organizing his room amused me. His phobia of sickness and every type of contagion, his chronic insomnia, melted me and made me want to protect him. The same happened to him with my obsessions, my fears, my own insomnia, and my constant frustration with my music. Still, I should say that it was also a time of great creativity. If I had noticed in my CD recorded months earlier in Copenhagen a certain stiffness, a certain horological precision, then now my music had more flow and greater presence. Not the strict vigilance of someone who fears making a mistake, but rather the abandon and spontaneity of someone who thoroughly enjoys what she is doing. There is, luckily, some evidence of that favored moment in my career. In addition to the recordings required by our host institution, I did three radio programs that I hold as proof of my greatest personal achievements. Laval conducted two concerts at the Royal Danish Theatre, both awe-inspiring. The audience gave him a standing ovation that lasted several minutes and, after the event, the musicians professed it had been an honor to share the stage with him. Having followed closely his development since then, I can attest that the month and a half he spent in that city marked one of the best—if not the very best—moments in his entire career. Yes, he established himself later on, but it is enough to listen to the recordings from those weeks to realize that within them there is an extraordinary emotional transparency.

Like me, Laval was married. Waiting for him in a chalet outside of Brussels were his wife and daughters, three blond, round-faced girls whose treasured photographs he kept in his phone. We preferred not to speak too much about our respective relationships. Despite what one might think, in that state of exceptional bliss there was no space for guilt or fear of what would happen later, when we returned to our worlds. There was no time but the present. It was like living in a parallel dimension. Whoever has not been through something similar will think I am coming up with these failed metaphors to justify myself. Those who have will know exactly what I'm talking about.

The residency ended in late September and we returned to our respective countries. At first it felt good to be home and to get back to our daily lives. But, speaking for myself, I did not return to the same place I had left. To begin with, Mauricio was out of town. A work trip had taken him to Laredo. His absence couldn't have been better for me; it gave me enough time to refamiliarize myself with the apartment and my normal life. It's true that, for example, in my study things were intact; the books and CDs in their places, my music stand and sheet music covered by a layer of dust barely thicker than when I'd left. But the way I was in my home, in every space and even in my own body, had changed, and even though I wasn't aware of it then there was no going back. During the first days I still carried on me the scent and taste of Philippe. More often than I would have liked they rushed over me like crushing waves. Despite my efforts to maintain composure, none of it left me unaffected. Once I'd given in to those feelings described, they were followed by those of being lost, of longing, and then by guilt for reacting that way. I wanted my life to go on as it always had, not because it was my only option, but because I liked it. I chose it every morning when I woke up in my bedroom, in the bed I had shared with my husband for over ten years. That is what I chose, not the sensorial tsunamis and not the memories that, had I been able to, I would have eradicated forever. But my will was an inadequate antidote to the pull of Philippe.

Mauricio came home on a Saturday at noon, before I'd been able to sort my feelings out. He brought me relief, like the boat you find in the middle of a storm that will save you from the shipwreck. We spent the weekend together. We went to the movies and the supermarket. On Sunday we had breakfast at one of our favorite restaurants. We told each other the details of our trips and the annoyances of our respective flights. In these days of reacquainting I wondered more than once if I should explain to him what had happened with Laval. It troubled me to hide things from him, especially things so serious. I had never done it before. I realized that I needed his absolution and, if it were possible, his advice. But I preferred not to say anything for the time being. Greater than my need to be honest was my fear of hurting him, of something between us rupturing. On Monday we both returned to work. The memories continued their attack on me but I managed, rather adeptly, to keep them at bay until Laval reappeared two weeks later.

One afternoon I got a long-distance phone call from a blocked number. My heart started beating faster before I picked up. I lifted the receiver and, after a brief silence, I recognized Laval's Amati on the other end of the line. Hearing him play from thousands of miles away, being in my own home, it tore open what I had tried so hard to heal. That call, seemingly harmless, brought Philippe into a place where he didn't belong. What did he want, calling like that? Probably to reestablish contact, to show me that he still thought of me, that his feelings for me still burned. Nothing explicit, and yet, so much more than my emotional stability could take. There was a second call, this time with his own voice, made, he said, from a phone booth two blocks from his house. He told me what his music already had: he still thought about us and was having trouble breaking free. He talked and talked for several minutes, until he'd used up all the credit he'd put in the phone. I barely had enough time to make two important things clear to him: first, everything he was feeling was mutual; and second, I didn't want him calling my house again. Laval exchanged phone calls for e-mails and text messages. He wrote in the morning and at night, telling me all kinds of things, from how he was feeling to what he'd had for lunch and dinner. He gave me reports on his outings and work events, on what his daughters were doing and when they got sick, but most of all—and this was the hardest part—he gave me in-depth descriptions of his desire. So it was as if the parallel dimension, which I believed to be suspended indefinitely, not only opened up again, but began to become everyday, stealing space from the tangible reality of my life, from which I became increasingly absent. Bit by bit I learned his routines, when he took his daughters to school, the days he stayed home and those when he went into town. The exchange of messages gave me access to his world and, by asking questions, Laval was able to open up a similar space in my own existence. I'd always been a person who often daydreamed but because of him this tendency increased dramatically. If before I had lived 70 percent of the time in reality and 30 in my imagination, that ratio did a complete reversal. It got to the point that everyone who came into contact with me began to worry, including Mauricio, who I suspect already harbored some notion of what was going on.

I was becoming addicted to my correspondence with Laval, to this interminable conversation, and to thinking of it as the most intense and essential part of my daily life. When for some reason it took longer than usual for him to write or it wasn't possible for him to immediately respond to my messages, my body exhibited obvious signs of anxiety: clenched jaw, sweaty palms, leg twitches. If before, especially in Copenhagen, we almost never spoke about our respective spouses, that restriction ceased to be enforced in a long-distance dialogue. Our marriages became objects of daily voyeurism. At first we only told each other about our partners' suspicions and worries; then about our arguments with and judgments of them; but so too about the gestures of affection they showed us to justify, to the other and to us, their determination to remain married. Unlike me, who lived in a calm and taciturn marriage, Laval was not happy with his wife. At least that's what he told me. Their relationship, which had already gone on for over eighteen years, had been for the vast majority of that time a living hell. Catherine, his wife, did nothing but demand his attention and intensive care and would unleash upon him her uncontrollable violence. It was unbearably sad to think of Laval living in such a situation. It was unbearably sad to imagine him, for example, stuck in the house on a Sunday, enduring the screaming and the accusations as the interminable Brussels rain fell outside. But Laval wouldn't think of leaving his family. He had resigned himself to living that way to the end of his days and I should say that that resignation, though incomprehensible, suited me. I didn't want to leave Mauricio either.

After three months of messages and occasional phone calls, we finally settled into a routine I felt more or less comfortable with. Even though my attention, or what remained of it, was on Laval's virtual presence, my daily life began to be tolerable, even enjoyable, until the possibility of seeing each other again arose. As I mentioned, every three months Laval traveled to Vancouver and on his next trip, post-Copenhagen, it occurred to him we could meet there. It would be easy enough for him to secure an official invitation from the school for me to lead a very well-paid workshop during the same days he'd have to be there that winter.

The idea, if extremely dangerous, could not have been more tempting and it was impossible to say no, even knowing that it threatened the precarious balance we had found.

So we saw each other in Canada. It was an incredible three-day trip surrounded once again by lakes and forests. The same thing we had felt during the residency again took root between us, only this time it was more urgent, more concentrated. We declined social obligations as far as it was possible. Whenever we were not working we were alone in his room, rediscovering in every way imaginable the other's body, the other's reactions and moods, as if returning to a familiar land you never want to leave again. We also spoke a lot about what was happening between us, about the joy and novelty this encounter had added to our lives. We came to the conclusion that happiness can be found beyond conventionality, in the narrow space that our familial situations as much as geographical distance had condemned us to.

After Vancouver we saw each other in the Hamptons; months later at the Berlin Festival of Chamber Music; then at the festival held in Ambronay for ancient music. Philippe had orchestrated every one of these encounters. And still, all the time we spent together was never enough for us. Each return was, at least for me, more difficult than the last. My distractedness was worse and much more obvious than when I came home from Denmark; I often forgot things, I'd lose the keys somewhere in the apartment, and, most terrible of all, it became impossible for me to live with my husband. Reality, which I was no longer interested in holding up, began to crumble like an abandoned building. I might never have noticed were it not for a call from my mother-in-law that drew me out of my lethargy. She had spoken to Mauricio and was very worried.

"If you're in love with another man, it's slipping through your fingers," she said to me with the bluntness she was known for. "You do whatever you have to to get it under control."

Her comment fell on absent but not deaf ears.

One afternoon Mauricio came home from work early to the sound of a Chopin piece for piano and violin that Laval had performed ten years before. A CD I'd never played in his presence. I don't know if it was the look of surprise on my face to see him home or if he had decided beforehand, but that day he interrogated me about my feelings. I wanted to give his questions honest answers. I wanted to tell him of my conflicts and my fears. I wanted most of all to tell him what I had been suffering. However, all I could do was lie. Why? Maybe because it pained me to betray someone whom I continued to love deeply, but in a different way; maybe I was scared of how he would react, or because I clung to the hope that, sooner or later, things would go back to the way they were. Mauricio's mother was right: I was losing my grip on the affair.

After turning it over in my mind, I decided to call off the next trip and put all my energy into distancing myself from Laval. I wrote to him explaining the state of things and I asked his help in recovering the life that was dissolving before my eyes. My decision upset him but he understood.

Two weeks went by without any kind of contact between Laval and me. However, when two people think constantly of each other there grows between them a bond that transcends orthodox means of communication. Even though I was determined to forget him, or at least to not think of him with the same intensity, my body rebelled against that plan and started manifesting its own volition through feelings, physical and, of course, uncontrollable.

I first felt a soft itch in my crotch. But when I inspected the area several times I didn't see anything and gave up. After a few weeks the itch, faint at first, barely noticeable, became intolerable. No matter the time of day, no matter where I was, I felt my sex, and feeling it inevitably meant also thinking of Philippe. I received his first message about it around that time. An e-mail, concise and alarmed, in which he swore that he'd contracted something serious, probably herpes, syphilis, or some other venereal disease, and he wanted to warn me so that I could take the necessary precautions. That was Philippe, *tout craché*, as they say in his language, and that was the classic reaction of someone given to hypochondria. The message changed my perspective: if we both had the symptoms, then most likely the same thing afflicted us both. Not a serious illness as he thought but maybe a fungus. Fungi itch; if they are deeply rooted, they can even hurt. They make us always aware of the body part where they have grown and that was exactly what was happening to us. I tried to assure him with affectionate messages. Before resuming our silence, we agreed to see doctors in our respective cities.

The diagnosis I got was just what I'd suspected. According to my gynecologist, a change in my mucus acidity had fostered the appearance of the microorganisms and simply applying a cream for five days would eradicate them. Knowing this did not calm me. Far from it. To think that some living thing had grown on our bodies precisely where the absence of the other was most evident astonished and rattled me. The fungus bound me to Philippe even more. Though at first I applied the prescribed medicine punctually and diligently, I soon stopped the treatment; I'd developed a fondness for the shared fungus and a sense of ownership. To go on poisoning it was to mutilate an important part of myself. The itch became, if not pleasurable, at least as soothing as the next best thing. It allowed me to feel Philippe on my own body and imagine with such accuracy what was happening to his. That's why I decided not only to preserve the fungus, but also to take care of it, the way that some people cultivate a small garden. After some time, as it grew stronger, the fungus started to become visible. The first thing I noticed was white dots that, upon maturing, turned into small bumps, smooth in texture and perfectly round. I came to have dozens of those little heads on my body. I spent hours naked, pleased to see that they had grown over the surface of my labia in their path toward my groin. All the while I imagined Philippe doing all he could, to no end, to get rid of his own strand. I discovered I was wrong when one day I received an e-mail in my inbox: "My fungus wants one thing only: to see you again."

The time I had before dedicated to communicating with Laval I now devoted to thinking about the fungus. I remembered my mother's, which I'd all but erased from my memory, and I began to read about those strange beings, akin in appearance to the vegetable kingdom but clinging to life and to a host, and cannot but be near us. I found out for example that organisms with very diverse life dynamics can be classified as fungi. There exist around a million and a half species, of which a hundred thousand have been studied. I realized that something similar happens with emotions: very different kinds of feelings—often symbiotic—are identified by the word *love*. Loves are often born unforeseen, of spontaneous conception. One evening we suspect their existence because of some barely noticeable itch, and by the next day we realize they have already settled into us in such a way that if it is not permanent, it at least seems to be. Eradicating a fungus can be as complicated as ending an unwanted relationship. My mother knew all about it. Her fungus loved her body and needed it in the same way that the organism that had sprouted between Laval and me was reclaiming the missing territory.

I was wrong to think that when I stopped writing to him, I would detach myself from Laval. I was also wrong to believe that that sacrifice would be enough to get my husband back. Our relationship never came back to life. Mauricio left discreetly, no fuss of any kind. He started by not coming home one night out of three and then extended his periods of desertion. Such was my absence from our common space that, although I could not help noticing it, neither could I do anything to stop him. I still wonder today if, had I tried harder, it would have been possible to reestablish the ties that had dissolved between us. I am certain that Mauricio discussed the circumstances of our divorce with very few of our friends. However, those people spoke to others and the information reached our relatives and closest friends. There were even people who felt authorized to express to me their support or disapproval, which angered me to no end. Some told me, as consolation, that "things happen for a reason"; that they had seen it coming and that the separation was necessary, as much for my own growth as for Mauricio's. Others claimed that for several years my husband had maintained a relationship with a young musician and that I should not feel guilty. This latter part had never been proven. Far from calming me, the comments did nothing but increase my feeling of abandonment and isolation. My life had not only ceased to be mine, it had become fodder for others' discussions. For that reason I couldn't stand to see anybody. But neither did I like being alone. If I'd had children it probably would have been different. A child would have been a very strong anchor in the tangible and quotidian world. I would have been attentive to the child and its needs. A child would have brought joy to my life with that unconditional affection I was so badly in need of. But besides my mother, who was always so busy with her work, in my life there was only the violin and the violin was Laval. When I finally decided to seek him out, Philippe not only resumed contact as enthusiastic as ever, he was even more supportive than before. He called and wrote several times a day, listened to my doubts, gave me encouragement and advice. Nobody was as involved in my psychological recovery as he was in those first months. His calls and our virtual conversations became my only enjoyable contact with another human being.

Unlike my mother during my childhood, I decided to remain with the fungus forever. To live with a parasite is to accept the occupation. Any parasite, as harmless as it may be, has the uncontainable need to spread. It is important to limit it, or else it will invade us entirely. I, for example, have not allowed mine to reach my groin, nor any other part beyond my crotch. Philippe has adopted an attitude toward me similar to mine toward the fungus. He never allows me beyond my territory. He calls my home whenever he needs to but I cannot, under any circumstance, call his. It is he who decides when and where we meet and who always cancels our trips if his wife or daughters mess up our plans. In his life, I am an infallible ghost he can summon. In mine, he is a free spirit that sometimes appears. Parasites—I understand this now—we are unsatisfied beings by nature. Neither the nourishment nor the attention we receive will ever be enough. The secrecy that ensures our survival often frustrates us. We live in a state of constant sadness. They say that to the brain, the smell of dampness and the smell of depression are very similar. I do not doubt it's true. Whenever the anguish builds in my chest, I take refuge in Laval, like turning to a psychologist or a sedative. And though not always immediately, he almost never refuses me. Nevertheless, as to be expected, Philippe cannot stand my neediness. Nobody likes to be invaded. He already has too much pressure at home to tolerate this scared and pained woman he has turned me into, so different from the one he met in Copenhagen. We have seen each other again a few times, but the trysts are not like before. He's scared too. His responsibility in my new life is weighing him down and he reads, even in my most innocent remarks, the plea for him to leave his wife. I realize this. That is why I have lessened, at the cost of my health, my imploring. But my need remains bottomless.

It's been more than two years since I assumed the nature of an invisible being, which barely has a life of its own, that feeds on memories, on fleeting encounters in whatever part of the world, or on what I am able to steal from another organism that I yearn for to be mine and in no way is. I still play music but everything I play seems like Laval, sounds like him, like a distorted copy nobody cares about. I don't know how long it's possible to live like this. But I do know that some people do for years and that in this dimension they are able to build families, entire colonies of fungi spread far and wide that live in secrecy and then one day, just when the infested being dies, raise their head during the funeral and make themselves known. That will not be me. My body is infertile. Laval will have no descendants with me. Sometimes I think I catch, in his face or the tone of his voice, a certain annoyance similar to the repulsion my mother felt for her yellowed toe. So despite my enormous need for attention I do everything I can to come off inconspicuous, so that he thinks of my presence only when he desires or needs it. I can't complain. My life is tenuous but I do not want for nourishment, even though it comes one drop at a time. The rest of the time I live locked up and motionless in my apartment where I have barely raised the blinds in the past few months. I like the dimness and the dampness of the walls. I spend a lot of time touching the cavity of my genitalia—that crippled pet I glimpsed as a child—where my fingers awaken the notes Laval has left there. I'll stay like this as long as he lets me, forever confined to one piece of his life or until I find the medicine that, at last, once and for all, frees us both.

The Snake from Beijing

My family, like many in this city, has diverse roots. Dad was born in China, but at two years old he was adopted by a French couple who brought him to Paris and raised him in their culture. They named him Michel Hersant, which is also my name. Mom, on the other hand, was born near Alkmaar in the Netherlands and grew up in a Protestant household until she was nineteen. She lived two-thirds of her life here and was able to completely lose her accent. What she never let go of was her culinary ways—she loved her bread and cheese and her good pastries—and her morals. As was the custom of her hometown, she left the curtains open to show the world that we had nothing to hide. My father didn't practice any religion. She was an actress, he, a playwright. They met in Latin America during the staging of a play he had written and in which she'd been cast as the lead. That was six years before I was born, that is, almost forty years ago. Since then they were never apart, except during the few times my mother went back to visit her country or traveled for work. Throughout my entire childhood and part of my adolescence my parents formed an indivisible block, a wall without a single crack against which it was impossible to rebel. More difficult for me than the mixing of origins and cultures was being the only child of a couple so fused together. I believe this union was the product of the very peculiar dynamic between them. Despite the love my grandparents showed my father, there was still something orphan-like about him. To him, his wife was another fake mother who was growing him, in his professional life as much as his love life, in a psychological uterus from which he'd never be expelled. Building this house in Montreuil had been her initiative, and it was her masonry skills, typical of Dutch women, that kept it standing for years. I'd always assumed they'd grow old together, in love: he increasingly Asian, gently watering the young plants in his garden; she baking pastries in her checkered apron like the plump little old women in fairy tales. However, there was a moment that cast doubt over all my assumptions. I, who had been intently observing them for seventeen years, started noticing in them alarming changes. Movements in the lives of human beings, according to an eminent Chinese oracle, begin below the surface, and therefore their origins are difficult to place in time. So I can't say exactly when the signs of discontent first appeared in my father's behavior. Nor do I know if it had always been there, dormant inside him, or if my mother and I, external catalysts, had caused it. What I can say is that as he aged he began to show an interest in his Asian roots he'd never had before, a kind of personal and secret quest he didn't want to share with us.

The change became evident after his first trip to China. An important theater in Beijing decided to stage *The Woman of the Link*, his most famous piece, and they invited him to oversee the production. As his name was French and his entire career had developed here, nobody imagined that the author of that very Western text would have their features and skin color. That trip dealt a heavy blow to my father's identity. His stay, which was supposed to last two weeks, was twice extended and ended up being a month and a half. According to him, he was learning a lot about himself and couldn't allow himself to return prematurely. What did he mean by that? He never really gave us an explanation. My mother and I thought he was trying to find out the whereabouts of his biological parents or, if they had died, the fate of other members of his family. But he proved our theory false when he came back.

Dad returned from Beijing noticeably affected. Not only was he all of a sudden fragile and withdrawn, but even his physical appearance had undergone a transformation. He had more gray hairs and had lost several pounds. But mostly it was the desolate expression that

rendered his face unrecognizable. Soon after he begin
building, all by himself, a study in our attic that from
the start looked to me and my mother like—as much
as he denied it—a kind of pagoda. It was the first time
I can remember that her eyes sought complicity in
mine. Her look was cheerful but also worried about her
husband's mental health; a worry I of course shared.
When he finished his study Dad moved most of his
books up there and did the same with those he later
acquired. His behavior made me think of emperors
buried with all their belongings in monuments built
solely for that purpose. Every book he bought after
that had to do with his new fascination; theater, nov-
els, philosophy, history, astrology, Confucianism, and
Buddhism, usually in English editions, were shipped
to our house and as soon as he took them out of the
box he brought them straight to his study. My mother,
at that point still humoring him, joked that her husband had entered a rebellious phase necessary for his
emancipation. What's true is that Dad didn't spend as
much time with her. Instead of talking to her at night
or rehearsing lines with her in their shared studio as he
used to, he spent hours locked up in his new refuge.
Seeing him so reserved and silent also reminded me
of monks who seek solitude in the mountains so that
they can meditate. However, my mother did not see
things in quite the same way. She soon abandoned her
tolerance and began fuming whenever he appeared in
the window of the pagoda, contemplating the evening
with the faraway look that never left his eyes anymore.

One Saturday morning soon after that Dad got in the car and left the house very early, without letting us know. When I saw the dismayed look on my mother's face, I had to stay with her and instead of going out with my friends like I always did I helped her make lunch. When he came back he had with him a terrarium in which we could make out the shape of a viper. He hastily greeted us as he walked by the kitchen door with his new purchase. There were too many changes in too short a time and we didn't know how to deal with them. We tried to interrogate him during dinner. Why did you buy it? What are you thinking of doing with it? Is it poisonous? Dad didn't give us a single good reason, only what felt like evasive answers about the snake being a healing symbol in the Chinese tradition.

That same evening my mother and I looked through the trash for all the information we could find about his pet. We discovered that he had bought it in a store a few blocks from the Les Gobelins metro station in Paris, its address written on the plastic bags. When Dad set up his snake in the pagoda I was afraid he was going to move up there to live with it. He'd spend hours sitting in front of its terrarium doing nothing but looking at it, so absorbed in his thoughts that he sometimes forgot to close the door. What was happening to him? Why, after having shared everything with Mom, was he excluding her from his search for his origins? Had he gotten tired of living in that Dutch womb? It was truly a mystery. Rather than hurt me, his incipient madness intrigued me. I started watching him through my binoculars every evening, looking from the kitchen into his den's only window. I wanted to know what he spent so much time on in that place he had built for no apparent reason and without respect for the house's original design. At first I held on to the hope that from his isolation a great creativity would emerge and flow into a marvelous play. But not once in all the times that I spied on him did I see him write a single line. Reading, that he did do, and when he wasn't doing that he was sitting in a chair watching the snake. He was a sorry sight.

Two Saturdays after that Dad again went out without telling us where. My mother searched his clothing for the pagoda key and found it. We took advantage of his absence to enter the place he'd never invited us. I remember Mom judging everything with disapproval and disgust, as if it were an assassin's lair rather than her husband's sanctuary. I can't say which was more noticeable in her expression, the disgust she felt or the sadness. I on the other hand gazed in curiosity at the objects Dad had accumulated in so little time: some blue metal balls, an etching of a yin-yang, Chinese coins, fabrics with dragon prints, a small carpet that looked antique. On his desk, the *Tao Te Ching* and *The Chinese Oracle of Changes*. It was all there, available and exposed, as if on display. I wondered if with all those symbols and esoteric texts he wasn't trying to summon his ancestors. The snake was, for me anyway, the most interesting thing there. It must have been about a meter long. Its brown skin had round, dark marks laid out in perfect symmetry. Mom and I stopped in front of the glass. It seemed to be in a deep sleep, coiled up in a corner of the terrarium. Though we tried, we couldn't find either its head or its face. I said to her, brightly so has to reassure her, that an animal so tame couldn't be dangerous. But she didn't agree with me at all and wanted to leave right away. After locking the door we put the key back and went downstairs. Mom poured herself a tall glass of whiskey on the kitchen table and summed up in a single phrase what she was thinking:

"The devil has entered our home."

She went on for a few minutes about vipers and their characteristics, as she understood them. Temptation, selfishness, evil . . . those things were my father, according to her. He carried all that inside him ever since he returned from China.

"Look at how skinny he is! I wonder if he started smoking opium. It would be terrible but at least we'd know what was going on with him," she concluded, leaving me stunned.

Monday, instead of going to school I decided to pass by the pet store where my dad had gotten his. The man and woman in charge were Asian, probably married, and middle-aged. I tried to speak with them without, of course, revealing my reasons for coming, but they could not have been harder to read. I pretended to be intent on buying one of their animals, and only then did they look at me with vague interest. After prowling past the aquariums against the walls, the fish tanks with turtles and chameleons, I asked them if they sold snakes. The man studied me in silence. I don't know why, but I got the impression that he was trying to guess my height and weight.

"We have them. Of course we have them," the woman replied. "It is our specialty."

They took me to a dark shed in the back room with artificial indigo lighting. I looked at the terrariums for a few minutes. In each there was a pair of the same species. The snakes were very different from one another. They varied mostly in size and color. Some had smooth skin that looked slippery. Others, however, had swollen scales that, as much for the texture as for the symmetry of the patterns, brought to mind a woven basket. The kind of plants and the intensity of the lighting changed with each habitat. I paused to watch an anaconda slowly eating a blue bird. It didn't discard anything, not even the bones.

"It is just an appetizer," said the man. "It could devour you when hungry."

I tried to stay calm and kept on walking. As I wandered the shed, I found a snake just like my father's and, just like his, it was sleeping.

"What species is this?" I asked the woman.

She slipped a piece of paper out from under the terrarium.

"Its scientific name is *Daboia russelii*," she replied. "It is found mostly in India, but in China it is known as a scissors snake."

"I like it," I lied. "It looks very tame."

She shook her head.

"They are very poisonous. As for their temperament, there are all kinds. Some of them are serene, others not so much. Depends on each animal. This specimen is not usually this calm. It's going through a bad time."

I wondered if this was a selling tactic. A boy looking for that kind of a pet had to want something more than an inert viper.

"She's in heat and last week her mate was taken away. They were very close. I urged the man who bought the male to take both of them. I even offered him a good deal, but he refused."

I looked at the paper she'd read from and saw the price: 1,500 euros. I thought of how much my father had spent since he'd come back from China. Just building his pagoda must have been several thousand. I looked a second longer at the snake and thought of how sad it must be without its mate.

I left the place with a heavy feeling in my stomach. My father's nostalgia for his country of origin had driven him to buy a piece of its fauna. Instead of going to class I went straight home. Dad had a meeting with a director friend of his from a foreign theater and I was sure that Mom would be happy to hear what I'd discovered. I was right to come home; as soon as I opened the door I found her drowning in tears and completely out of her wits. She didn't ask me about school and got straight to the point:

"Your father has a lover. An Asian woman he met on his trip. I told you that animal was a sign of misfortune. I don't know what to do, thank goodness you're here."

I decided not to tell her that I'd been to the pet shop. Instead I suggested we go to her favorite pastry shop on the other side of the city. An absurd idea that she readily agreed to. She was in such a state of shock that I think she would have gone along with anything I suggested. Once in the café, in front of a chocolate Sachertorte that she looked at as if it were a stone, she told me what she knew and how she'd learned it.

That morning, as soon as my father left for his meeting, Mom went into the pagoda and looked through his online accounts. Dad had been basically handicapped with those kinds of things for many years and Mom had handled his e-mail. She found in his trash folder two compromising photographs with dates matching his trip.

"Her name is Zhou Xun," she told me. "She's an actress and, naturally, very young."

Based on what she told me, in one of the photos my dad was with her in some scenic spot. The typical shot taken on a cell phone while out walking. In the second they were smiling, barely dressed, in what looked like a kitchen in an apartment. Both their names were on the bottom of the photo along with the dates. My mother was convinced that the actress was the one who had taken them and had promised to send them to him. Mom bemoaned her luck for an hour, not touching her cake. She listed all the sacrifices she'd made for him since the time they'd met, everything she'd done to turn him into the prestigious playwright he was today, to keep him protected in a stable home, centered around him and where he'd always had the leading role. Things obvious to both of us, and I'm sure to my father as well. She confessed to me how disappointed she was by his infidelity, and when she grew tired of feeling sorry for herself she returned to the subject of his pet.

"That animal is diabolical, I've said it many times before. I want to ask you to get rid of it."

"Why don't you kill it yourself?" I asked. But she wouldn't.

"If your father finds out, I think it will be easier for him to forgive you."

Mom was convinced that the snake was the incarnation of her marital troubles. She had put her entire life into that marriage. How could I refuse her request? I took her trembling hand and promised that she could count on me. She let out a heavy sigh, after which she began to eat slowly, like a good little girl whose punishment had just ended.

I suggested we go home a different way so we took the metro from Gaîté. We got off at Edgar Quinet and cut through the cemetery, walking in silence over a carpet of dead orange and yellow leaves. As I always did when I passed through, I examined the inscriptions on the headstones, the cities and dates carved into the stone, the occasional epithet. I thought how in the end all that is left of us besides our name is two dates and two cities, if not one city as in my case it could be. It was impossible to know where my father would die and where he would be buried, but one thing was certain: under his name would be written *Beijing, 1953*.

I wondered if Mom was thinking the same thing, but she looked so lost in her own thoughts that I decided not to ask. A few minutes later she dispelled my doubts on her own.

"If you look closely you see that most of the women are buried next to their husbands. There are few women alone in this cemetery."

I realized that she was scared of being buried apart from my father.

"There's Sartre and Simone de Beauvoir's grave," she added, her tone that of someone who has just discovered something interesting. I looked at the headstone she was pointing to: dark letters carved onto a white surface. You couldn't say they'd been an orthodox couple. For years they lived in a love triangle and had bloody fights. But still, look at them. There they are, buried like any other husband and wife.

That afternoon, after I'd already promised to destroy the snake, I swore to her that come what may, I'd bury her in the same place as my father.

"It's fair," I concluded. "All those years aren't invalidated just because of some teenage girl."

A few feet away I found two gray headstones engraved with gold lettering in Chinese and French. A very large family lay in each.

"Maybe I'll also fit near you," I said to her. "Why bury only two when so many bones fit inside a single grave?"

My mother never again mentioned what we'd talked about that afternoon. When we got home she made dinner like she did every night and went back to being her old self, or at least she seemed to. I on the other hand carried on my shoulders the weight of my two promises, especially the more immediate one.

Before going to sleep I searched online for more information about my father's snake. I learned that *Daboia* is the name of the genus to which the five poisonous snakes of India belong. In Hindi the word means "that which lies hidden and lurking in the darkness." I thought of his lover in Beijing. I then began investigating the risks of living with these animals. I discovered that their venom contains neurotoxins that block respiration; their victims die of asphyxiation. A single bite can be lethal if the correct antidote is not administered immediately. What was Dad, whom I'd always thought of as a rather cowardly man, doing with one of these creatures in his study? Placing this threat a few feet from his family, barely separated from us by delicate glass, was like activating a time bomb. Hadn't it been enough to endanger us with his Chinese romance? Mom was right. We had to get rid of the creature. But how? At that point I hadn't the faintest idea. I was going over it in my mind all night and I came up with a few options. The first—the most humane—was to release it in the park a few blocks from the house. Then I realized that it might bite me when I tried to pick it up, whether I meant to hurt it or free it, and I didn't want some child finding it behind a bush or on the wooden handrail. Another risk, though less probable, was that Mom would find out and accuse me of betraying her. I then thought of poisoning it. It was the cheapest and easiest way. The only danger was that my father would find out and blame me forever. I decided to risk it. The next day after school I went to a gardening store and asked how I could kill a snake I had spotted in my yard. They recommended a substance, apparently very effective, and I took some home with me. I hid it in the top shelf of my dresser, waiting for the right time to go up to the pagoda.

In the meantime, I kept looking into his study window with my binoculars. One afternoon I found my father consulting the *I Ching*. It wasn't something unknown to me. He and Mom had always had one in their studio and whenever someone suggested a new theater project they flipped the coins to find out what they could expect. However, as strange as it may seem and even though it was a Chinese book—perhaps the Chinese book par excellance—I'd always associated it more with my mother. She was the one who usually tossed the coins on the table. That afternoon Dad's face in my binoculars was serious and yet serene. Though I tried, I couldn't even imagine what he had asked. Nor was I able to focus on the book well enough to read its response. My father read in front of his computer the pages that corresponded to his hexagram. He then left the book open and stood up. He walked a few steps to where the terrarium was and sat down and watched his snake for a long time. My mother, who had been cooking right next to me this entire time without speaking, called out a few times that dinner was ready and after

several minutes of silence we heard Dad's slow foot-
steps coming down the stairs. In the little he spoke that
night, he mentioned that Friday morning he'd be going
to the Chinese embassy. Through a very close friend
he'd managed to get a meeting with a senior official
to discuss the whereabouts of his parents. Mom and I
looked at each other in surprise. I remember—and it
still pains me, how this went—that Dad tried to look
me in the eyes and I had to look away.

"It should matter to you a little bit," he said to me.
"They are your relatives too."

I was about to respond by saying that I knew perfectly well who my grandparents were and I didn't need
any more, but Mom, in her typical restraining way,
rushed in.

"I think it's wonderful what you're doing, and I'm
sure Michel does too."

I only smiled to show I supported her.

Friday morning, when Dad went off in search of his
past, I took the jar of poison and asked my mother
for the study key. She reached into her pants pocket
and took it out. I realized that she had been expecting me. She watched me unlock the door but this time
she didn't cross the threshold. As soon as she saw me
approach the terrarium she ran back downstairs. The
first thing I did when I went in was read the page of
the *I Ching* that my father had left open on his desk. It
was on hexagram number twenty-nine. The unfathom-
able, the abyss. I read the following: "In man's world,
K'an represents the heart, the soul locked up within the

body, the principle of light enclosed in dark—that is, reason. The name of the hexagram, because the trigram is doubled, has the additional meaning, 'repetition of danger.' If you are sincere, you have success in your heart, and whatever you do succeeds." It felt like the text was speaking to me more than to my father. I heard the sound of the gate. It was too early for him to be back but I thought he might have forgotten some document, so I looked out of the window to check. I saw my mother leaving, as she always did, to go to the local market that took place every Friday morning. One of the lines of the hexagon was underlined in pencil on the page. "Six in the third place means: Forward and backward, abyss on abyss. In danger like this, pause at first and wait, otherwise you will fall into a pit in the abyss. The nobel son should not behave badly."

I stopped reading and sat down on the chair where Dad sat every evening watching his *Daboia*. I told myself that keeping an animal like that was the same as keeping a loaded gun in a drawer: a means to escape the world within arm's reach. The animal seemed more alert that morning than usual. I noticed a dish of water in the habitat that I didn't remember seeing the last time, and determined it was the perfect place for me to empty the jar of poison. But before I did, I decided to wait a little. The words of the *I Ching* were still dancing around in my head. It was then that I heard my father's steps on the stairs, giving me just enough time to hide the jar under the seat.

He didn't ask me what I was doing there. Nor did he

seem upset. He looked at the *Oracle* open on his desk and hazarded:

"I gather you've already read the response."

There was something about him that bewildered me in a way I cannot describe. The man standing in front of me had my father's voice and face; he smelled like him and made many similar movements, but at the same time, something about that person made him a complete stranger to me.

I felt like I should justify myself; I don't know exactly what for, perhaps for my intrusion or for what he'd read about me in the pages of the *I Ching*. "The noble son should not behave badly."

"Mom told me you have a lover."

"That's exactly what I wanted to talk to you about."

With those slow steps he had been taking ever since he'd come home, Dad walked over to the desk and took out two printed photographs. The same ones my mother had found in the trash folder.

Written on the back of the image were the girl's name, mailing address, phone number, and e-mail.

"That's her. Look at her closely."

She was indeed a very beautiful woman and several years younger than him.

He told me he had fallen more in love with that woman than he'd ever been before, so much so it made him feel ridiculous because of the intensity as much as years that separated them. Zhou Xun wasn't even eighteen. He also told me that it had been impossible for him to resist.

"It was an emotion as lethal and sudden as a snake-bite," he confessed to me. "I think of her every second of the day. However, what your mother said is not true. We are not lovers. We were for five weeks, while I was in Beijing. She was counting on me to get her out of China, but since I've come back I've given her no sign of life. According to your own ancestors, the only way to get rid of a demon or an afflictive emotion is to face it. That's why I bought this animal, that's why I decided to separate it from its mate, to observe its pain as a reflection of my own."

"And what about your marriage?" I asked.

"Your mother is also my own," he answered. "I've returned to her because I belong to her, but I'm not who I used to be, and thus I cannot give her what I did before. I don't know if I'll always be like this. Right now I feel like this animal you want to poison: a lifeless life."

I thought again of my father's grave. If what he said was true and it went on indefinitely, the second inscription on his headstone could read: *Beijing, 2012.* In which case Paris, where he had lived for most of his existence and I want to say the most important part of it, would be left off his grave. Dad himself told me that in China the snake is a symbol of healing and the continuation of life. In the spring it sheds its skin and it is as if it's been reborn. Adult children fulfill this same function. They ensure the continuation of the story that began with their parents.

"I know it was your mother who asked you to destroy

my snake. You owe her your loyalty and I will not stop you. In exchange, I want you fulfill my obligation to Zhou Xun. Choose the moment you want to, but do it. It is nothing less than a debt, what I left unfinished with her."

Dad went over to the sofa and picked up from the floor the jar of poison I'd hidden. Not even looking at me, he poured a little of the dark liquid into the habitat, drawing the shape of a triangle. Then he asked me to leave his study.

My mother never found out about that conversation. When she came home I only assured her that the poison had been given. Several days went by before the snake stopped moving, and when at last it did my father still did not remove it from his pagoda. The Chinese symbol of renovation remained motionless in his study for many months until the day Mom took it out, without warning or rationalization, terrarium and all. Despite what she'd firmly believed, getting rid of the snake was not enough to resuscitate her marriage. My father never saw another springtime. Instead of regaining his liveliness or at least returning to his old ways, he sank deeper into the grief that defined the final years of his life. The *Daboia* that he brought home never did harm us. The snake from Beijing, however, left him with a wound that no home remedy was able to heal.

About the Author

One of the most talked-about writers of new Mexican fiction, Guadalupe Nettel has won the Radio France International award for best new writers from non-French-speaking countries, the Gilberto Owen National Book Award and the Antonin Artaud Award for her collection of short stories *Pétalos* (*Petals*), and the Premio Heralde and the Anna Seghers Prize for her novel *El huésped* (*The Guest*). For years she has contributed to a number of French- and Spanish-language literary magazines such as *Lateral, Letras Libres, Paréntesis, La Jornada Semanal, L'atelier du roman*, and *L'Inconvénient*. Her books have been translated into French, Portuguese, German, Italian, Dutch, Czech, Slovak, and Swedish.

In June 2013 Granta featured Guadalupe Nettel in their "Best Untranslated Writers" series. *Natural Histories*, for which she won the 2013 Ribera del Duero Short Fiction Award, and her novel *The Body Where I was Born* (Seven Stories Press, 2015) are her first books to be published in English. She lives in Mexico City.

About Seven Stories Press

Seven Stories Press is an independent book publisher based in New York City. We publish works of the imagination by such writers as Nelson Algren, Russell Banks, Octavia E. Butler, Ani DiFranco, Assia Djebar, Ariel Dorfman, Coco Fusco, Barry Gifford, Martha Long, Luis Negrón, Hwang Sok-yong, Lee Stringer, and Kurt Vonnegut, to name a few, together with political titles by voices of conscience, including Subhankar Banerjee, the Boston Women's Health Collective, Noam Chomsky, Angela Y. Davis, Human Rights Watch, Derrick Jensen, Ralph Nader, Loretta Napoleoni, Gary Null, Greg Palast, Project Censored, Barbara Seaman, Alice Walker, Gary Webb, and Howard Zinn, among many others. Seven Stories Press believes publishers have a special responsibility to defend free speech and human rights, and to celebrate the gifts of the human imagination, wherever we can. In 2012 we launched Triangle Square books for young readers with strong social justice and narrative components, telling personal stories of courage and commitment. For additional information, visit www.sevenstories.com.